Cole

Hathaway House, Book 3

Dale Mayer

Books in This Series:

COLE: HATHAWAY HOUSE, BOOK 3
Dale Mayer
Valley Publishing Ltd.

Copyright © 2019

ISBN-13: 978-1-773361-55-0
Print Edition

About This Book

Welcome to Hathaway House, a heartwarming military romance series from USA TODAY best-selling author Dale Mayer. Here you'll meet a whole new group of friends, along with a few favorite characters from Heroes for Hire. Instead of action, you'll find emotion. Instead of suspense, you'll find healing. Instead of romance, ... oh, wait. ... There is romance—of course!

Welcome to Hathaway House. Rehab Center. Safe Haven. Second chance at life and love.

When Navy SEAL Cole Muster entered Hathaway House weeks ago, he was doing well. His meds were under control; his recovery was progressing at a safe rate, and he was getting better every day. But, left to his own devices, Cole pushed himself too hard and took himself off his medication—and ended up causing himself harm and earned himself time in a hospital. Now he's returned, hoping that Hathaway House can get him back on track one more time.

RN Sandra Denver feels responsible for what happened to Cole. She was his nurse and should have realized that he wasn't ready to leave Hathaway House. His setback was her fault, or at least she could have prevented it, if she'd made sure he was taking those meds she gave him daily. Now that he's back, she's finding it hard to trust not just him but herself. And she understands, when Cole has a hard time trusting himself too, it won't make his recovery any easier.

For Cole's sake, Sandra must help him overcome his

stumbling blocks as well as her own. With any luck, they'll find a second chance at recovery, for both of them, at Hathaway House.

Sign up to be notified of all Dale's releases here!

https://smarturl.it/DaleNews

Chapter 1

C OLE MUSTER LEANED against the headrest of his hospital bed at Hathaway House and stared out the window. Acres and acres of verdant green pastures cordoned off with white fencing met his gaze. He couldn't imagine how many acres were here, but he assumed at least forty, and that meant the property alone had cost a ton of money. Several horses grazed nearby, and even a goat bounced through the various paddocks. Outside his window was a stunning picture. After being in a sterile city hospital room for too long, this was a luxury.

A luxury he'd lost—temporarily anyway. A luxury he wouldn't take for granted again.

He realized now how much he'd been fighting to get back here before he nearly lost it all. That he was given one more chance brought a sense of relief almost overwhelming in its intensity.

He understood what the doctors here had said about his setback. Something about too much stress, a swelling bladder, too much exertion, sleeplessness due to the onset of PTSD and the abrupt cessation of his meds. They didn't even mention his initial injuries. Then they did tests, inserting catheters and whatnot, all over again.

And just like that, he was back at that city hospital, almost in tears when he woke up there. He'd been terrified he'd lost his one chance at Hathaway House. Of attempting that miracle recovery he'd heard about from friends—which he so desperately wanted for himself.

Depressed was too minor a word for his mood—*devastated* was more appropriate. The doctors had promised he could return to Hathaway as soon as he stabilized. At the time he hadn't believed them, but now as he looked around his bright, cheerful cream-colored walls and tiled floor, with that beautiful expanse of horse pasture outside the window, he believed. And he'd do anything to stay. He'd only been here for a couple hours, but he just wanted to lie in bed and rest, regroup after his travels and remind himself never to take this place for granted again.

Yet, he was petrified to do too much and end up in the hospital a third time, essentially banning him from Hathaway House. Overdoing it was what had done him in the last time. He'd been so determined to meet up with Brock again, to set some serious goals, to make a life for himself that Cole thought he had to give it his all and do as well as his friend had, or he'd lose the prize—getting his health and strength back and losing this damn wheelchair.

He had been so cocky and so sure of himself that he had *chosen* not to take several of his medications and had worked to exhaustion with disastrous results. The cumulative effects had spiraled quickly, his body shutting down various vital functions, resulting in an ambulance ride to the hospital.

He wouldn't make that costly mistake again. As someone who'd survived BUD/s training and spent six years as a SEAL, Cole knew exactly how damaging mistakes could be. He hadn't been ready to walk away from his military career, but being in a truck when a landmine blew up was a hell of an exit strategy. He'd been flung free and then speckled with shrapnel. He'd lost the lower half of his left leg. After that, infection set in and required several more surgeries. Now he had an outrageous-looking purple-and-red stump that, so far, refused to accept any weight on it.

He looked forward to increased mobility and knew that eventually enough scar tissue would form so he could use a prosthetic limb, but right now it wasn't an option. He had also taken a hit with all the bits of shrapnel in his back and shoulder, plus his landing had broken his hip. Thankfully his sciatic nerve, although bruised, hadn't been badly affected. But it'd been painful as hell.

Recovery was a bitch, but that was why he was here—to strengthen his back and to get his hip fully functional again. Then, of course, there was his leg and shoulder. Crutches worked but not for very long and not for very far, yet he felt like using the wheelchair was giving in, even though it was easier on him.

Cole had always had more than his fair share of stubbornness. But he also had more than his fair share of fear, and that still bothered him because one of his biggest fears facing him now concerned his future. He had no idea what he would do from here on out. He could probably return to the military and take a desk job. But once you'd been at the top, office work wasn't really an option. He had several friends who'd left the service to work at private security companies, but they weren't a busted-up, beat-up, old piece of shit like he was. Every time he thought about holding down a job or of eventually being independent, his mind shut off, and his fear took over.

Still in denial mode, he couldn't face it all yet.

He'd had hopes and dreams growing up, but they had all been focused on the military. And he'd worked steadily to make that happen. Now he had no idea what to do for a second career. The thought made his gut bubble with acid.

He took a deep, ragged breath. Time to get this show on the road. As his mind took that leap, he heard footsteps in the hallway. Sure enough, they stopped at his door, and then there was a light rap.

"Good morning, Cole."

He smiled at Dani, the manager of Hathaway, who'd been nothing but gracious regarding his ultimate failure at his first launch. What if his second was just as bad?

He tried to drop that kind of thinking, sitting up straighter, and smiled at her even more brightly.

She walked in and studied him.

He could feel this most critical test—the assessment of his health. She might not be a doctor, but she was hell on wheels as a first-alert system.

"Glad to see you're awake, Cole, after your transfer here. It's almost lunchtime. Good timing on your part," she said with a big grin. "I believe the chefs are doing a Greek-themed meal today."

"That sounds wonderful. I am pretty hungry," he admitted.

"That's a good sign." She lifted her tablet and jotted some notes.

Curiosity flared in him. He knew he wasn't allowed to see what she wrote, but that didn't stop him from wanting to know. Besides, notes would be a part of life here. They would all keep track of his condition, including her.

"Your team will drop by this afternoon," she said with another smile. "We'll take this morning as a complete reboot."

He brightened. "I was hoping you'd say something like

that," he confessed. "I felt quite the fool for having made a mess of my first time here."

"Don't feel like a fool about anything. But please remember, it's very important that you follow your plan exactly. You do have medications, and you do have exercises, and you do have very important meetings to attend." She patted his hand gently. "If you are concerned about anything, then first and foremost, discuss those issues with your team."

Abashed, he nodded again. "I'm sorry. I didn't mean to cause so much trouble last time. I thought I was doing so well, and I got cocky."

"It's nice to see you were feeling so positive and enthusiastic," Dani said, "but it's very important that you don't do too much, too fast. Your rehab plan is put in place for a reason. You need to trust your team to know what's best for you."

He winced. This was probably the first of many recriminations he would have leveled at him, especially once his team arrived. "I've learned my lesson." He turned to stare out the window. "I promise it won't happen again."

"Good. So, a few changes have been made in your team because of some staff shifts and patient discharges, not because of what happened earlier." She handed him a sheet of paper. "These are your team members. Once again, everybody will stop by this afternoon and say hi. Not until after lunch though. If you have any questions, you can talk to them or me."

Once more she studied him for a long moment. "I can get someone to take you out in a little bit. But not on your own power today."

"Good." He smiled at her look of surprise. This was the

new him. Careful. Someone who listened to instructions and his body. "I am tired. I'm not sure my legs feel up to it." He glanced around the room. "If I can't get around, do I call for somebody, or should I get into the wheelchair on my own?"

"Today, somebody'll help you."

He laughed. "Fair enough." He glanced at his watch. "Do you think I could text Brock and ask to meet him today?"

She beamed a beautiful, bright smile. "He would like that." She turned and made her way to the door. "Sit tight. I'll send somebody in right away."

SANDRA DENVER CARRIED her now-empty medication tray back to the pharmacy. She carefully locked up the tray as she did every time. She took one last look around the room, then pocketed her keys. It was almost lunchtime. So far, the morning had been routine. It wouldn't stay that way though.

Cole was back. That was enough to send butterflies flitting through her stomach. Initially she had been attracted to the man, but she was also furious at him. She knew she shouldn't take it personally. If he hadn't wanted to take his medications, then that was his right. He was a legally consenting adult.

But he'd signed up to follow the programs here.

She was also following his doctor's orders. She'd been the one to give Cole the medications and to trust he would take them. When he hadn't done so, without letting everyone know, she'd felt responsible.

Even now, this burning red ball of rage was in her. She'd received a verbal upbraiding from the doctor, and she'd taken it as she did everything—with a stoic expression and an apology. Afterward an unknowing innocence had disappeared. Up until then, it had never occurred to her that people here might hide something from her, like not taking their medications. But from now on, no way could she be complacent about her patients' actions.

Since that day, when Cole had been rushed to the hospital, she took an extra five minutes with each patient, ensuring all their medications were completely swallowed before she left the room. Many of them objected. Quite possibly she should have been double-checking all the time, but people came here voluntarily and signed up and paid big money for their recovery. All they had to do to make a change in their medications was talk to their doctor. She wasn't in charge of that.

As she walked into the main hallway, she caught sight of Dani coming toward her. "Good morning, Dani."

"Morning, Sandra." Dani tilted her head toward the dining room. "On your way to lunch?"

Sandra nodded. "That's exactly where I was heading. I'm looking forward to the souvlaki and whatever else the kitchen made today. The last time we had Greek food," she said, "you had to get there fast before it was all gone."

"Well, I believe the chefs are doubling the amount today," Dani said. "But you're right. He who is late gets only leftovers." She turned and looked down the hall. "Would you mind helping Cole into the dining room? He's planning on meeting Brock for lunch."

Sandra stiffened and tried to cover her reaction. "Brock's a great guy," she said warmly. "I can do that."

But something must have been in her voice because Dani turned suddenly and studied Sandra's face. "Cole's been a slightly disruptive presence since he arrived, but he's trying to make this second transition as smooth as possible. If this is a problem, please let me know."

Sandra would have to face him eventually—this would be a relatively easy way to break the ice. She shook her head and forced a smile. "I'm fine. I'll go get him. I presume we're taking the wheelchair?"

Dani nodded. "Yes. He's not ready to walk with his crutches yet."

With that, Dani continued toward the dining room. Sandra took a deep breath and turned resolutely in the direction of Cole's room. He was damned lucky Dani had let him return. After that stupid stunt of his, Sandra would've shot his ass back to the VA hospital and left him there.

Chapter 2

S ANDRA APPROACHED COLE'S bedroom slowly. The door was open, which was a good sign. She knocked and stuck her head in. "Hey, Cole."

Cole turned to look at her. He smiled. "Hey, Sandra."

"You're looking better."

He grimaced. "Be hard not to, considering the shape I left this place in the last time."

"Not taking your medicine will do that to you." She couldn't resist saying that. His shamefaced look made her realize she'd been hanging on to something he probably wasn't. Everyone always thought they knew better. It was something she dealt with daily. "I met Dani in the hallway. She asked if I'd make sure you meet up with Brock for lunch."

He straightened, almost as if insulted. "I'm sure I can get there on my own."

"I'm sure you could too. But not today. It's very important you start off as slow as you can." She waited. "So is that a yes or a no?"

He nodded. She guided the wheelchair to his bedside and watched as he slid to the floor on his good leg, grabbed the wheelchair arms and shifted his body into the seat. She walked around to the front and adjusted the footrest for his leg.

"You may want this," she said, grabbing his lap blanket and throwing it onto his lap.

He tossed the blanket back to the bed. "I hate the blanket. It always makes me feel like an invalid."

She sighed. "In that case, the blanket can stay here, but if you get cold ..." She let her voice trail off in warning. "Remember, no lack of communication of any kind this time, please." She pushed him toward the door.

Normally he'd be strong enough to wheel himself to the buffet, but they would all be watching him closely for the next couple weeks. It was incredibly easy to overexert, particularly when accommodating the loss of his lower leg. Plus, his body was still dealing with the surgical aftermath from his most recent time in the hospital. His medications had also been increased, and he tired easily.

She didn't want him to be so exhausted he couldn't get back to his room. He was stubborn enough that he wouldn't ask for help and would do it alone anyway. She'd seen pigheadedness in all its forms here, and it usually came from the men. Something about the male ego didn't like asking for help. She could understand that, but sometimes egos had to be put in check.

"I'm ready for lunch myself," she said. "I hear it's Greek today."

"I didn't have a chance to try the food that much last time. My visit was so damn quick."

"That's too bad, because the food is great around here. They never skimp."

"And for you guys too, right?" Cole craned his neck to look up at her. "The staff eats here also, don't they?"

"Oh, absolutely, we do. It's one of the perks of working here."

"I imagine there are a lot of those. Brock told me about the pool, but I never made it there."

"There's the pool, the food, the horses and living accommodations for those of us who might need them. Yes, there are a lot of advantages to working here."

He nodded. "I thought so. Is the environment always so happy? Everyone seems so upbeat all the time. That's very unusual."

"That's because it's a good place to be." She pushed him through the entrance of the large dining area. "Did Brock tell you where he would meet you?"

"I never thought to ask. I forgot how big this room was."

"I'll take you to the deck so you can sit in the sunlight, and we'll look for him as we go." She pushed him out to the deck where the sun was high enough to produce some good heat, but not be unbearable quite yet.

There was no sign of Brock as they made their way to the far end of the deck. "Maybe you're early."

"Maybe." He kept twisting and turning in his seat to look for his buddy. "He said noon. He should be here by now."

Sandra understood how Cole felt. "Once he shows up, I can either fix a plate for you or you may want to see all the offerings on the buffet line. Let me know." As she settled Cole at his chosen table, she heard someone call out.

"Cole."

There was Brock, making his way over—smooth, agile, and stronger than Sandra had ever seen him before. She caught Cole's reaction—the whisper of envy on his face—and felt a rush of sympathy for the man. She patted his shoulder. "Don't forget. He's been here for a few months now. You'll get there."

He glanced at her and said in a low voice, "Well, I'd be damned happy if I end up looking like how Brock is now. He was more broken than I was."

Unbidden, a gentle smile made its way to her lips. His eyes held hurt and fear, and she was damned sure he wouldn't want to know she'd seen either.

"I'll bet you on it. You follow your regimen and listen to your team, and it won't be long before you'll be like him."

Brock threw his arms around Cole and gave him a big hug. "Damn, it's good to see you again." He sat and stared at Cole, a big grin on his face. "Man, I was afraid you weren't ever getting back to this place."

"So was I," Cole admitted. "You don't know how happy I am to be here."

Brock grabbed Cole's hand. "This is the best place. You'll be a whole different man by the time you're done."

"I hope so. I was admiring how well you're doing. I didn't expect to see you looking so healthy and fit."

Brock laughed. "Well, there is the physical side, and there is also that lovely healed emotional side."

When he caught that particular grin on Brock's face, Cole studied him for a moment. "Don't tell me you've found a woman too?" He didn't want to sound as shocked as he felt, but damn, he was shocked. He shook his head. "Only you, dude. You come to a place of healing for a bunch of broken-down old farts, and you end up with a partner. Talk about luck."

Sandra rolled her eyes at the macho banter and then watched Sidney walk toward them, carrying two cups of coffee. Sandra would be leaving Cole in good hands now with Brock and Sidney.

Sidney stopped beside Brock and looked at Cole. "Ready

for round two at Hathaway House?" No malice was in her voice, only sympathy and a touch of gentle teasing. She shared a telling look with Sandra.

Cole winced visibly. "Could we forget about round one? That would be really good if we could."

Sidney put the two cups on the table and said, "Considering you're Brock's buddy, maybe. Maybe, just for you, we'll let all that slide." She faced him squarely. "You probably don't remember me, but I'm Sidney."

Cole shook his head. "I don't actually. Sorry."

Sandra looked at Sidney, a smirk on her lips. "He had just commented on the fact that Brock found a relationship in a place like this."

Sidney laughed, pink washing over her cheeks. "It was touch-and-go for a while there, but we made it."

Sandra saw the questioning expression on Cole's face as his gaze went from Sidney to Brock and then back again. When he glanced at Sandra, she nodded. "Yes, it is possible."

He dropped his gaze to the wheelchair and his partial leg. "Maybe for some people."

Cole's mutterings caught Sandra's ear. She walked away then. Cole would need time to adjust. He also had to shake off some of his self-pity and his downcast attitude. Brock had done a lot of work to get into the condition he was in. It was important Cole saw that effort for what it was—effort he would have to put in himself, at a pace his own body could handle. There were no shortcuts to this.

However, with Brock's rehab months ahead of Cole, maybe he would use that as his inspiration to move forward. She certainly hoped so. Cole had the ability to completely turn around his life. This place had so much to offer, as he'd said. She'd like to see him ready to take on the challenge. But it was all about mind-set.

His mind-set.

She wasn't sure he was there yet.

COLE WATCHED SANDRA as she walked away. Her attitude had changed over the last few minutes. He hadn't been as sure of his welcome when he had met her earlier. She'd been friendlier with Sidney and Brock. He remembered what she had said about his medications, and for the first time considered how not taking his medications might've affected more people than just him. He'd taken the physical hit ... but maybe she had too in another way. Right. She had probably gotten into trouble.

Goddammit. That was not what he wanted.

No wonder she hadn't been as friendly when she came to his room.

"Hey, buddy, what are you thinking about?"

He turned his attention to Brock. Bigger than life and looking like he had a whole new lease on it.

"You are looking incredibly well." Cole shook his head. "I hope my recovery is just as good."

"It will be, but it's not easy. You've got to put in the work but not overdo it. Find the right balance." Brock grinned at him. "And having Sidney as my trainer didn't hurt."

"Hey, I'm not a personal trainer. I'm a physiotherapist," she said to Brock. Then turning to Cole, she added, "He likes to put me into the gym-model role regardless." She shook her head. "Talk about demeaning, Brock." Her light and happy tone belied her words. Sidney rose then. "You guys can talk all you want, but I'm hungry. And I've got to get back to work in an hour. Time to get some food."

Cole watched as she walked away. "Hot damn, Brock. She's dynamite."

Brock settled back with a satisfied smile on his face. "Yes, she is. But believe me, it's more than just looks. She's got a huge heart, and it's all mine."

"You are one lucky guy."

"Lots of women are here. Maybe you'll find one for yourself." Brock looked toward the buffet. "Sidney is right. We need food." He hopped to his feet. "Are you freewheeling, or do you want a hand?"

In that moment—that one sentence with no judgment, only acceptance—he knew Brock did understand what Cole had gone through and what he still had to go through. And he knew Brock wouldn't judge him for not getting there on his own.

"If I want to stay on Dani's and Sandra's and Sidney's good sides, then I could use a hand. I promised I'd do as little as possible this morning," he admitted. "And that includes wheeling myself around here."

Brock chuckled. "It's important to not get on anyone's bad side here," he said. "Come on. Let me do the honors. You'll be running around this place in no time."

"Lord, I hope so. I'm just worried about doing too much again only to land in the hospital." He lowered his voice. "You said it yourself. You were afraid I wouldn't return. Well, I'm terrified that, with one wrong move, I'll be kicked out of here forever," he admitted.

"That would suck," Brock said, his voice equally low. "So we have to make sure you start the right way and build on that. These are good people here. Give them a chance. They'll do right by you."

Chapter 3

S ANDRA HEARD THE last part of Brock's advice. She hadn't planned on sitting so close to them, but by the time she had filled her lunch plate and had found a table of her own, there wasn't much choice. She had been forced to sit closer to them than she'd wanted, and their voices carried. Still, it was good advice Brock had handed out. Hopefully Cole would use it. She could see he had the makings of a decent, and probably wise, man. Everybody was out of their comfort zone when it came to major health issues. How people reacted during a crisis said a lot about who they were inside.

She'd seen grown men cry in despair, and other men showed such inner strength and character through their adversity. This place had it all. Yet, what you arrived with didn't mean that was what you were stuck with. Being here transformed people, or rather they transformed themselves. The patients had a lot of support at Hathaway House, but it was up to them to take the required steps. That was what she wanted for Cole. Originally Brock had been one angry person too. Then Sidney had gotten hold of him. Even before they had started their relationship, she'd shown him what he could do if he put his mind to it.

That was the difference, having an entire team working on a patient's care, and Sandra was a part of Cole's team. She wasn't a therapist—she wasn't someone who had an active hands-on role to play. She was a nurse. She came to see people on a daily basis, but she was one of a lot of people not just working with one or two patients. Three permanent full-time nurses were on staff, and then they had several aides who came in on a part-time basis and that was just the day shift. Everyone still had plenty of work. There were dressings to be changed and stitches to be checked, and there were often catheters and other various physical issues to be attended to. She was happy to do it. She enjoyed her work.

The medication rounds gave her nightmares now. Amazing how one incident, such as Cole's, was enough to underscore she'd not been as diligent as she should've been. She was lucky that something much worse hadn't happened before. Now it woke her up in the middle the night, chilled and sweating, the "what ifs" running endlessly through her mind.

When she was alone and in the dark, and no one else was around to hear, she often found herself crying in fear. She never wanted to be responsible for the deterioration of somebody's health. She was always extremely careful with her medication distribution. It was one of the areas that had been really impressed on her throughout her training. She'd had a mentor through all the years she'd worked in hospitals, and they'd always stressed the same thing. She'd been here for four, maybe five years now, and a situation like that had never come up—until Cole.

Oh, she'd had her own various struggles. She'd had people who argued with her, not wanting to take a specific medication. That was fine. She had them talk to their doctor. She only adjusted the medications as per the doctor's instructions.

But to have someone, like Cole, deliberately fake taking his medication to avoid letting anybody know what he was doing—well, that was scary. She hoped he'd learned his lesson, and she knew she certainly had. These days her rounds took longer because she waited for people to swallow their medication in her presence. Several had commented on it. She half expected somebody to complain, but so far, nobody had—or none that she'd heard of.

The complaints may have stopped at Dani's door. Sandra should probably find out. Better to know up front than to wait for a second complaint to come through.

She finished off her lunch, having successfully blocked out the rest of Brock and Cole's conversation, and carried her dishes to the busboy's cart. She smiled at Dennis, one of the kitchen staff, standing near the buffet. "Dennis, that was absolutely fantastic. I'm all for Greek food every week."

"You're not the first to say that."

"How about we go global? Take a two-week period and pick a country and then do something different every day?"

He laughed. "I can mention it to the chefs, but they've got their own ideas too. Although I honestly think you will like what they've got planned."

"I know I will. What you guys end up doing is awesome." With a smile, she picked up a cup of coffee, snagged a cinnamon bun—which she didn't need but couldn't resist—and headed toward Dani's office.

Dani looked up and smiled. "Hey, Sandra, how are you doing?" Her gaze dropped to the cinnamon bun. "Oh, my God, that looks absolutely fantastic."

"I know, but it's way too damned big." She asked Dani, "You want half?"

Dani glanced at her, then back at the cinnamon bun

wistfully. "I shouldn't ..."

Sandra stepped in, closing the door behind her with her foot. "Neither should I." She sat, split apart the cinnamon bun and picked up her half, nudging the plate closer toward Dani. The two women sat in secret enjoyment and polished off the treat.

"By the way, the Greek lunch today was absolutely divine," Sandra said.

"It was, wasn't it?" Dani licked her fingers and then reached for her coffee cup to help wash down the dessert. "I wanted that bite of something sweet. Thank you." Dani focused on Sandra, her eyebrows raised. "Is there a problem? Did you need to talk to me about something?"

Sandra shook her head. "No problem. I wondered if there had been any complaints about me."

Dani's expression turned to surprise. "No. Should there be?"

"I guess I deserved that." Sandra laughed and reached for a napkin on the desk to wipe her fingers. "Since Cole's slip ... I stand by to ensure patients actually take their medication now." She shrugged. "I felt horribly guilty when he deteriorated so quickly. I couldn't figure out what the hell was going on."

"That wasn't your fault though," Dani said. "Cole brought that on himself."

Sandra nodded. "Oh, I totally agree. But it doesn't make me feel any less responsible."

Dani tossed her pen on her desk and leaned back in her chair. "That's the thing about living at this place. We're not responsible for everyone else's actions. We live with these people. We watch their growth. We see their failures. It's damned difficult sometimes." She stared out the window.

"Learning to separate guilt and responsibility, placing it firmly on the head of the person where it belongs, can be a challenge."

"I agree. I just wondered about any complaints," Sandra confessed. "I try to be super nice about it. I bustle around to make myself useful, but I am always watching like an eagle to make sure they pop those pills. A couple people have commented on it."

"Have they? Well, they don't appear to mind that much because nobody's been to see me." Dani sank in her chair a little deeper. "Most patients here are very amiable. Every now and again, we'll get somebody who's much less so, but so far, I haven't heard any complaints."

Sandra bounced to her feet and picked up the empty plate off Dani's desk, relief flooding her body. "That's good to hear. I won't pester you any longer. Have a nice afternoon."

"You too," Dani said. "Thanks for the treat."

With a big smile on her face, Sandra headed back to her office, feeling much better until she found Kenneth, one of the more troublesome patients, in the staff offices, studying the whiteboard with this week's schedules. What Cole did was harmful to himself. But what Kenneth did was harmful to others.

"Kenneth," Sandra said, "you are not allowed back here. This is for medical personnel only. The door is clearly marked."

"You have a weekend off coming up. I'll take you to town for dinner, a movie ... a nightcap. Breakfast on Sunday morning."

"No, Kenneth. I don't date patients."

Thank God Shane showed up right then as Kenneth did

not take her rejection well. Shane seemed to understand what was going on. He patted Sandra's back but his focus was on Kenneth. Motioning toward the door, Shane said, "We've talked about this before, Kenneth. Your lack of respect for boundaries. Your inappropriate behavior with the female staff."

"It's not like that," Kenneth said. "Sandra and I are dating."

"Stop it," Shane said with authority, his voice loud.

"Kenneth, that's a lie. We are not dating," Sandra said, happy to hear more footsteps coming their way.

"Like I told you before, Kenneth, only male staff will interact with you because of your treatment of the female medical personnel here. Now I'll have to report this latest incident to Dani." Shane shook his head. "This was your second strike. If you continue with these unacceptable actions, you'll be banned from Hathaway House."

By this time Dani and Stan and a couple male orderlies had appeared.

"I didn't do anything wrong," Kenneth shouted as he was led away.

Sandra shuddered. Kenneth was the one patient in hundreds that was difficult. And all because he wouldn't follow the rules. She couldn't wait until he left.

"I THINK I'VE shown you everything on the top floor." Brock stopped and stepped slightly in front of Cole. "Are you up for more? I can take you downstairs and show you the vet's clinic and out by the pool, or I could take you back to your room."

Cole tried to assess his condition. "I *am* a little tired, but I'd love to go downstairs. If I can see it all today, that will give me something to work toward. I saw a little the first time, but I'd been so focused on getting better I never paid any attention to my surroundings."

"Good enough." Brock pointed the wheelchair at the elevators. After he pressed the button, one of the elevator doors opened immediately. He pushed Cole inside and sent the elevator down again.

"There are stairs here too for your use later in your recovery," Brock said. "A challenge you can set for yourself is to make it to the animals or the pool on your own power."

Cole chuckled. "I like the way you think. I should get a notebook or something, so I can write down some of these ideas."

"If you don't have one, Dani's got some she keeps in a filing cabinet."

"I hate to ask."

"If you have a problem asking, I'll get you one."

The double doors opened, and Brock wheeled Cole from the elevator. "We'll take a right and go to the veterinary clinic. Probably a couple human patients are inside and easily a dozen furry ones. Everybody, patients and medical staff alike, come here whenever we need that connection. You like animals, don't you, Cole?"

"Absolutely, especially dogs." Cole watched with interest as they entered the veterinary clinic's waiting room.

The vet was saying goodbye to a customer leading away a golden Lab. "Hey, Brock. How's your day going?"

Brock smiled. "It's going awesome. This is Cole." He turned toward Cole and said, "Cole, this is Stan. He's the vet here."

"Nice to meet you, Cole."

"Nice to meet you too. So, according to Brock, we're allowed to see some of the animals?"

"Absolutely." Stan turned. "For that matter, I've got someone you should meet." He came back a moment later with the biggest, fluffiest critter Cole had ever seen.

"It's white, and it's huge. I have no freaking idea what it is, but I love it," Cole said with a laugh. It was placed in his arms very gently. He wrapped his arms around the creature and hunted for its face.

"What is it?" Brock asked, fascinated.

"It's an Angora rabbit. One of the longest haired ones I've ever seen. His name is It, after the character on *The Addams Family* show."

"What's wrong with him?"

Brock and Cole were busy petting the animal, whose ears could now be seen, followed by a pink nose. The rabbit lifted his head and sniffed. Cole laughed. "Keeping this guy clean has got to be a full-time job."

"He's actually a show animal who had trouble with a couple of his claws, so I gave them a good clip and disinfected one toe that was looking like trouble."

After a moment of holding the rabbit and enjoying having an animal in his arms, Cole lifted him up and handed him back to Stan. "I'm a dog person," he said, "but I've never spent much time around other animals to know if I like them or not."

"Stick around here long enough and you'll get lots of opportunities to find out." Stan held the rabbit carefully in his arms. "Anytime you want to go outside and spend some time with the horses, feel free. Just make sure to tell the staff where you're going and for how long, and also don't open any gates if you can avoid it. Slip through the fences or climb over the top instead. If you have to open a gate, make sure you close it really fast behind you."

Cole smiled. "Sounds fantastic. I won't be taking any chances with gates for quite a while, but just the thought that I could even go out there ... now that is something to strive for."

Soon afterward Brock steered Cole's wheelchair down the long hallway and through a door to the outside. "In this direction, we have access to all the pastures and the horses. There are times," Brock admitted, "that Sidney and I come here for picnics. It's a great spot to sit outside and eat."

It seemed like way too much effort for Cole now, but the concept brought a smile to his face. "It's nice to know it's a possibility too."

Brock moved the wheelchair in the opposite direction. "I'm taking you this way, so you can see what the staff uses after hours, and we can too in our private time, and during therapy."

As they approached, Cole could hear laughter and splashing. "Is this the pool you were talking about?"

"It is."

Suddenly, there it was in front of them. Cole gasped. "Wow, it's huge," he exclaimed. "I didn't expect to see anything this size."

"That's because it's for therapy and fitness. So it's got some serious lane length. I'm not even sure how long it is, but I wouldn't be at all surprised if it wasn't twenty-five yards. Although it's probably closer to twenty."

Cole studied the beautiful blue water. "Half is under cover?"

"Yes, that makes it the best of both worlds." Brock continued to push Cole alongside the big patio. A couple people sat off to the side, having coffee. "This is open to everybody, but only once a patient is cleared to come. There is no lifeguard on duty. So most need an orderly and that means part of the therapy."

"That makes sense. A lot of people here are not in the best physical shape. Accidents do happen." Cole studied the ramp at the far end. "The ramp's helpful too, I'm sure."

"Yeah. Be careful around it though, and you're only allowed in the pool after the doctor okays it and you've advanced enough to handle yourself." Brock took his buddy around one edge of the pool. "I've never seen it in operation, but there is a lift here to help some patients into the water."

"Thankfully that's not my problem."

Brock squeezed Cole's shoulder. "I hear you. I wasted a lot of time in bed, thinking about how shitty my life was and how stupid my accident was. Now I look around, and I think, damn, I'm in great shape."

"I need to remember that. I'm feeling stupid about everything I did in my first attempt. Now I just want to reboot and move forward and make a go of this."

"Then you can. But you must depend on your team. Let them know you're working with them because they're working for you. If one of you gets off track, well, it can get ugly." Brock kept them moving around the swimming pool, past a hot tub, and then around the far side. "We'll head all the way around to the ramp out front," he said. "After the tour, I'll take you back upstairs."

"How does the food work again?" Cole should know this, but he'd forgotten.

"There are always drinks and snacks available. If you're hungry, you can ask for food. Otherwise, it's three meals a day. Breakfast from six to nine, then lunch from eleven until one, I believe—although I've been there later, one-thirty, even two o'clock, and had no problem getting food. Dinner starts at five and runs until seven."

"Good. I'm looking forward to that. One of the worst things about being in the hospital was the food."

"You're right. That was *the* worst." Brock laughed. "That won't be your problem here." He pushed Cole up the front ramp, and before Cole knew it, they were at the double doors of the entranceway. Brock rolled the wheelchair onto the large Welcome mat and waited for the glass doors to open automatically. Instantly, cool air hit them.

Cole nodded at Melissa manning the front desk.

"Good afternoon. Giving Cole a tour," Brock said.

Melissa smiled at the two of them. "Good afternoon to you two."

Brock left soon after they returned to Cole's room as he had a meeting with his doctor to check on his own progress.

Moving carefully, Cole got from the wheelchair to his bed and was damned grateful to lie down and collapse. Who knew how tiring sitting up could be? Inside, he felt a hell of a lot better. This place offered so much more than he had first thought.

Cole had dozed off when there was a rap on his door. He opened his eyes to see a tall man walk in with a tablet in his hand.

"Good afternoon. I'm Dr. Herzog. I stopped by earlier, but apparently you were out and about, having a social hour."

No recriminations were in his voice, but it reminded Cole he and the doctor were both probably on a schedule.

"Sorry. Brock took me on a tour of the place. I understand I have a schedule around here somewhere, but I haven't had a chance to settle in yet."

"True enough. But after the last time, I don't want to delay your rehab too long, so that you get in the shape you need to be in. Are you ready for an exam?" He raised an eyebrow at Cole.

Cole rolled over and nodded. "As ready as I'll ever be."

Chapter 4

SANDRA NEARED COLE'S room as the doctor walked out. She waited for him in the hallway. "How is he?"

Dr. Herzog smiled. "He's in the best shape we've seen so far. I'm feeling quite encouraged, but it's his turn now."

She sighed with relief. "That's good news. I was a little worried we'd have another repeat."

He shook his head. "I don't think so. I've noticed a strong shift in attitude. He has a lot more gratitude about being here now."

"I'm glad to hear that."

"I'll go over the changes in his medication with you now, Sandra. We'll start him on the first round this afternoon."

She nodded and checked his tablet and then pulled out her own. Together they synced the medicine and dosage information and updated Cole's file.

"Okay. I'll make the changes on his next dose. He should be in meetings all afternoon."

"Yes, he should be, but he's been out and about this afternoon, so he's missed a couple. I had to circle back to see him. I'm the first one to touch base with him," Dr. Herzog commented. "We need to be on this."

"I took him down for lunch, and the last I saw of him, he was with Brock. I'll go over Cole's schedule with him and make sure he's doing okay and he didn't do too much on his first day back," Sandra said.

"You're the one who insisted on the wheelchair?"

She nodded. "And Dani."

"Good. It'll take him a couple days to adjust. He has to build up that leg and his arm too, not focus only on his back."

"The surgical scars don't look all that great either. Did you notice?"

"Yes. I noted a small amount of inflammation, but I've given him a topical ointment to put on daily, so with any luck, the redness and swelling should soon go down." With that, Dr. Herzog smiled and headed off to see his next patient.

Sandra tapped on the door.

"Come in."

She walked in, stopping near the bed. "Hey, Cole. Where did you and Brock go?"

Cole looked up and smiled at her. "We went all around the compound. It was good. I really like that pool."

"Hey, this is Texas. Everybody likes pools."

He chuckled.

"The doctor gave you your checkup," she said, "but I need a baseline set of measurements, like blood pressure, for example, and to run you through a standard checkup for my own records."

He lay back with his tablet on his belly. "Do what you need to do."

That was a change in his attitude. He hadn't exactly been this easygoing before. In fact, he'd clearly not seen the point. He'd wanted to start his physiotherapy right away. She was happy to see this compliance. "Did you see the animals outside?"

"Outside and inside." He smiled up at her. "It's quite a place."

"It is, indeed." She ran through her checklist, marked down his results and added a few notes about his attitude and general condition. "You need anything else this afternoon?"

"No, I believe I have people who I'll be seeing later."

"Yes, you will. Your tablet should have your schedule of appointments on it. Let me know if there are any problems."

"I will." He glanced over at the bedside table. "I forgot to get a cup of coffee to bring back to my room. Is that something I can get on my own at any time?"

"As far as your team allows you. For now, I'll grab you a cup. Cream or sugar in it?"

"Thanks, I like it black though."

She nodded. "Back in five."

It was not part of her duties, but she'd always found it a simple thing to be nice to people. Besides, if it kept Cole in bed a bit longer, then that was fine with her. Her instructions were to keep him as calm and low-key as possible, so grabbing a cup of coffee was not exactly a hardship.

In the dining hall, Dennis was cleaning up after lunch. She snagged a coffee cup from a fresh tray of hot mugs that he'd set down and then took another one for herself.

She made her way back to Cole's room and found him almost nodding off. She tiptoed inside and set the cup on the table, turning to leave.

"I'm not sleeping. Honest."

She chuckled. "You could have fooled me. It looks like you were two *Z*s away from being gone."

"It's a shock to see how tired I still am," he admitted.

"I think one of the biggest challenges for the big strapping young men when they arrive here is to recognize the limitations of their bodies. Major illness and trauma are hard to adjust to. However, this isn't forever. This is what you must deal with for the moment. Every day it will get better and better."

On those words, she tiptoed out again. Hearing no response, she figured he'd fallen asleep, but he called out after her, "Thanks."

She smiled. "You're welcome."

Maybe it *was* a completely different Cole this time, and that was a good thing. She headed to her office to update files before she saw her next patient. That was one of the things about her job—there was always paperwork. She started with Cole, taking the opportunity to write down a few additional observations she'd realized since leaving his room. These were notes she kept for herself, but his doctor could read them as well.

She'd come to trust her own judgment when it came to patients, until the incident with Cole. Thankfully Dr. Herzog had come to trust her judgment too. One of the reasons why she liked working here. She never felt like her opinions had no value.

In fact, it was just the opposite. She felt the doctors had come to rely on her quite a bit. She never wanted that to be taken the wrong way or for their trust to be misplaced. Not ever again.

AS MUCH AS Cole tried to brush it away, Sandra still seemed less open than last time. That was too damned bad because he really wanted to know her better. It had never occurred to him that she might have gotten into trouble over him. If she had, then he needed to apologize for that. However, at the same time, he wanted to move on, to move forward and to forget about his first attempt to stay at Hathaway House.

He studied the cup of coffee beside him. The best way to make it up to her was to do well this time. He knew more team members were due in this afternoon. He shifted on the bed until he was sitting up, leaning against the headboard. He wished he had a notepad. He still preferred paper and pen over his tablet. And Brock was correct. Cole needed to make some goals. He pulled out the phone he'd been given and was happy to see it was similar to the one he'd had here before. All the same contacts were in there, and he'd already added Brock.

He dialed Dani's number, and when she answered, he said, "Brock suggested you might have a notepad for me to use to write down a few goals and notes to help me do things a little differently this time."

"Absolutely. I'll be your way in a few minutes. Any idea which size you want?"

The question surprised him. He had been hoping for something to write on, not anything specific. "No, just something you don't need. Even a few pieces of paper would be helpful."

"I'll find something for you," she said.

With that call ended, he put down his phone and lifted his coffee.

Shane walked in as Cole set down the cup again. "Hey, Cole. I don't know if you remember me, but I'm Shane Roster. I met you the last time you were here."

Cole nodded. "You're my physiotherapist?"

"Absolutely." He placed his tablet on the end of the bed. "I saw you getting the tour from Brock, and Dani's given me her word you were warned not to overdo it these first few days."

Cole chuckled wryly. "As much as I'd like to forget about the last time, it appears everyone wants to keep reminding me."

"Only for today," Shane said with a smile. "We have to make sure we're all on the same page. It's good timing too. The notes just came through from your last hospital visit." He opened his tablet again. "You've been doing a series of exercises, but you're struggling with the stump. Is that correct?"

"The lower part of my back and my left underarm were damaged by shrapnel," Cole admitted. "That makes crutches very difficult."

"So, you'll be in the wheelchair for a while as that stump heals, and you're prepped to get a prosthetic limb on it as fast as possible. Then we'll get you on two crutches until you can handle just one as you adjust to your prosthesis. Ultimately you won't require crutches at all. Mobility is one of the greatest joys and rights of the human form." Shane glanced at Cole. "Obviously this will be an awful lot of work, and you need additional help to stabilize your frame. Some of the muscle tissue is gone forever, and we can't do anything about that, but your body will compensate. Particularly if you lean sideways for prolonged periods or for any repetitive movement that you do. So we must ensure that you don't fall into that trap." He studied him. "Case in point is the way you're sitting right now. Close your eyes and tell me how you feel in terms of balance."

Cole closed his eyes and tried to assess where the pressure points were. "It feels like I'm leaning to the right and the headboard is hitting hard on my right shoulder. There's pressure on my right hip, more than on my left."

"Now open your eyes and look at the way your body is sitting and leaning. See it from my perspective."

Cole opened his eyes and frowned. "It *looks* like I'm straight. So why does it *feel* like I'm so much heavier on one side?"

"Because you're still subconsciously protecting your injured left side. Now, while you're looking at me, imagine yourself with your body as you were before your accident. Equal muscles, both sides strong, both toned, and then shift your seating accordingly."

Cole frowned. "It sounds odd, but … I have to close my eyes to do that."

"Then close your eyes."

He shifted his weight in his mind, seeing his body as it once had been. Entirely strong, he prided himself on his left and right sides being equally balanced. He'd been a gym junkie and worked his left side extra hard to match it up with his dominant right side. In his mind, he saw his body as it used to be, and he used his hands to shift his position and then leaned against the headboard. He opened his eyes. "Is that better?"

Shane walked over and picked up a small mirror from the top of the dresser. He held it up, and Cole stared in surprise. "I swear to God, I shifted over." But it wasn't visible.

"That's because, in your mind, you still can't trust your body to keep you from falling. Imagine sitting in the middle of a bed surrounded by cushions and then shift your weight so you're sitting upright, using the mirror."

Cole shifted and leaned until he sat straight. He shook his head. "I feel like I'm falling."

"That's a trust issue. You must get to where you can do this without having to consciously think about it. But imagine if you spent your whole life leaning to the right, even when you're sitting in bed and propped up. Imagine what happens to the muscles on the right and to the muscles on the left."

Cole winced. "Yeah, not a pretty picture. I used to do a lot of bodybuilding," he said. "It was hard to get the two sides to match."

"Obviously you're right-handed, so a lot of work had to be done to balance out the left side."

"Right. So, is it a mental impression that I'm not secure or am I really not getting it?"

"It's both. Your perception is of having an injured left side, and you don't trust it can hold you. That's what we'll work on." Shane put down the mirror.

"It's a bit of a relief," Cole said, "because it's quite a shock to see how much I'm protecting that side."

"That's why I want you to do this, starting today, for ten minutes of every hour that you can." He looked at his watch. "Over the next five hours or so, sit in this 'uncomfortable' awareness position for ten minutes of every sixty. Then go back to what you were doing. You must retrain your body to understand this current position is natural and what you've been doing before is not natural. But you can't do it all at once. It becomes easier and easier as we slowly build up the muscles on the left side."

He made a few more notations on his tablet, and then he said, "I'll be back to see you in the morning. Have a good afternoon."

As soon as he had left, Cole shifted into his usual position. "That was at least ten minutes," he muttered.

Yet, he could see what Shane was saying. It was a little disconcerting. Why the hell had nobody mentioned that before?

Cole had known he had to get back here. These people would help him. He felt like the last place had been overrun with underpaid staff. Although the hospital people had cared, they had so many to tend to that damned little got done. Cole didn't want to be mollycoddled. He didn't want somebody to pat his hand and sympathize. He wanted somebody to kick his ass and push him to step forward.

Like what Brock had. That's what Cole wanted for himself. He wasn't sure that Shane would be that kick-ass guy, but he had already noticed something that nobody else had while Cole had been hospitalized.

And that was a damned good thing.

Chapter 5

WHEN HER DAY was done, Sandra got yet another cup of coffee. She should probably cut back—just as she and Sidney had said all too often—but for whatever reason, she drank more caffeine than she liked. Habits were hard to break. Instilling new healthier ones were more difficult. Case in point, she had yet to address her fear of water, or maybe it was a lack of confidence in her swimming skills, even though her on-site apartment was only steps away from the magnificent Hathaway House pool. Shaking her head, she took the stairs to see Stan and the animals. She'd heard talk of a large Angora rabbit but didn't know if it was still here.

Besides, she hadn't been to the vet clinic for a couple days. She felt better when she visited on a regular basis. There was always a dog or a cat that needed a cuddle.

Nobody was at the front desk, and nobody was in the waiting room. She frowned and checked her watch. Normally Stan was still here. Sure enough, the door opened then and Stan walked out. He took one look at her and smiled. "Hi, Sandra. How are you doing?"

"I was feeling a little on the blue side, and I hoped to hug an animal ..." she said, her voice trailing off.

He opened his eyes wide and smiled. "How about me? Will I do?"

With a big grin, she stepped into his arms and hugged him. Stan was like a resident big brother. Although he was only fifteen years her senior, there was nothing other than friendship between them. As far as she knew, he had never had a relationship with any of the staff here either. She wasn't sure how she felt about relationships between staff, but she figured that if the two people were consenting adults, it was nobody else's business. However, if it did affect the work environment, then that would change things.

"There was talk of a very large rabbit?"

"Did Cole tell you about that? Yes, that was It. He's back home already, but I'm sure you can visit the ones still here."

She brightened. "That would be nice."

He led the way into the back, and thankfully, most of the surgical recovery cages were empty.

She glanced at the sedated dog with tubes running in and out.

Stan noticed where her attention was and nodded. "That's Jojoba. He had a tumor on his hip I removed. He'll be fine though." Stan walked to the rear wall where the cats were. A big mama cat and her kittens were in the same cage.

"Oh, my gosh! They're so tiny."

"She was brought in pregnant. So now we'll keep her until the kittens can be weaned. Although, if I find a foster family, that would be good too. We'll find homes for the babies and fix the mom, so she doesn't end up in this situation again."

Sandra didn't want to take one of the babies from its mother. She glanced around. "No other dogs or anything?" She shook her head and smiled. "Quiet day for you."

"Exactly. Have you been out to see Molly lately?"

She shook her head. "Molly? Not sure I've met her at all," she confessed.

Stan laughed. "Let me show you." He took her through the back way and out the side door. He pointed. "There." The little filly raced up and down the meadow near the two older mares. "Molly's the baby."

They walked to the fence, and all three horses came over right away. Stan kept a plastic container at the corner. He opened it up and pulled out a handful of grain, which he gave, open-handed, to the older two. Sandra did the same for the baby.

"Oh, my God, she's adorable."

"Innocent and fresh, with the whole world ahead of her. Sometimes we have to remember that."

"I know. It's easy to forget that, isn't it?"

"Sounds like you've had a rough day."

"And yet, I didn't. I do seem to be in a down mood though."

Stan nodded. "Sometimes we don't need a reason. Sometimes the color of the sky is just gray, not blue. Sometimes there is no laughter, just talking. That doesn't make for a bad day. It just makes it another day."

She grinned. "Words to live by."

COLE STARED AT the four walls of his room. Overall, his day had been good. However, keeping his energy expenditures to a reasonable amount, he still wanted to get out for a bit. He wasn't sure how anybody would react to that, but if he took his wheelchair, maybe it wouldn't be too bad. He was tired, but it was doable. Even to sit by the pool would be nice. It was hot today, and the air-conditioning blew through the room, but it gave him a closed-in feeling. He wanted sunshine and warmth, but at the same time, he didn't want to be in the killing heat. The pool might be a good answer. He'd love to get in the water, but he knew he wasn't allowed to do that yet. And he sure as hell wouldn't go against anybody's wishes. This time.

Maybe Brock was up for it. Cole sent his buddy a text message. **Hey, interested in going to the pool or sitting outside somewhere?**

Absolutely. Be there in five.

Perfect. Even if they just grabbed a cup of coffee. Although, he seemed to be slugging that back pretty hard. He was sure other choices were available at the coffee bar or in the buffet line.

It wasn't long before he heard Brock's footsteps coming down the hallway. Cole managed to sit up, and using the headboard as he had done before, he sat in the wheelchair. He smiled at his buddy. "I hope you don't mind. The walls were closing in on me."

Brock nodded in understanding. "They do that real fast here." He stepped up behind Cole's chair. "Where would you like to go?"

"I was thinking the pool area because it would be cooler but still out in fresh air."

"That's possible. But there are also the animals. How about we take a walk around and look at the horses first?"

"You sure you're okay pushing me?"

"Hell, yeah. Sidney's got me on some pretty awesome strength-building exercises. My back and shoulders are stronger and better than they've ever been before," Brock said. "I can't wait for you to feel the same thing, buddy."

Cole wanted the same damn thing so bad. He also knew that going too far, too fast … "I do too. All in good time."

"That's the attitude." Before long, Brock had them downstairs and outside in the fresh air.

Cole tilted his face to the waning sun. "It's beautiful here. I haven't seen so much green grass in one place."

"Something to do with the underground springs. Water in Texas is worth its weight in gold. Hathaway seriously has an incredible irrigation system, but I imagine—in the hot, dry season—it can get pretty tough to water all this."

"Isn't that the truth? Still it looks like pictures of Kentucky."

"Agreed." They wandered the grounds in silence.

The majority of the grounds surrounding Hathaway was wheelchair accessible, to make it possible for all the patients to get around outside easily. As they walked to one of the pastures, a goat ran alongside them and jumped on the top railing of the fence.

"I gather they're not trying to keep *them* inside," Cole said.

Brock laughed. "Not sure you can."

Cole studied the goat—it was very small, almost pygmy size. But it was friendly. It jumped off and came to visit. Cole reached down and gave it a good scratch behind its ears. The goat jumped up and landed in his lap. Cole laughed.

"Is that okay, or do you want me to take him off?"

Cole laughed again. "Nah, it's good. I don't remember the last time I had a goat in my lap."

He wrapped his arms around the fuzzy creature and gave it a hug. The goat *baaed* at him and jumped off.

"I guess he didn't like the hug much."

That little touch of nature in its purest form put a lightness of spirit back into Cole he hadn't even realized he lacked. He and Brock stayed and watched the goat as it danced and pranced and jumped along the fence. A moment later, an older goat called to it, and the baby took off.

"Was that a kid or a pygmy?"

"I have no idea," Brock replied. "All I can tell you is that it's very active." He grabbed Cole's wheelchair and pushed forward again. "There are the horses." He pointed out the big ones, and then Cole saw the little one.

"Hey, another baby."

"Yeah, that's Molly."

Cole listened as Brock told him what he knew about the little filly's history.

"They tried to keep her as a pet? Why would people do that?" He stared off at the obviously contented horse, eating grass and sticking close to the two bigger horses. "And the other horses?"

"One is Maggie, who's been here since forever. She was a rescue. I'm not sure about the history of the other one," Brock admitted. "Dani also has her own horses here. Midnight's on the far side by Dani's house, and I think she has another one also. Of course they are all hers essentially."

"There's a house on the property?" Cole twisted to look but couldn't see anything.

"Check the tree line and look closely." Brock pointed to the left.

Then Cole caught sight of it. A beautiful house nestled, almost hidden, in the trees. "Wow, that's nice. Is that hers?"

"Her father owns all this. He built this business up from nothing. The Major had a lot of adapting issues from his own military injuries when he bought this place, and he and his daughter built it up as much for his own project as to help others. Have you met the Major yet?"

Cole shook his head. "Not that I remember." He cast his mind back, and then an older man with white hair, a white beard and a big smile came to mind. He'd gone from table to table in the dining room, busy talking with everybody. "I think I know who you're talking about though."

"If you haven't met him yet, you will soon. The Major delights in getting to know everybody here. This place is more about family than being an institution."

Cole could see that. "If he's beaten back his own demons, then he'll have a good idea what everybody else is going through. It's not easy sympathizing or empathizing when you can't relate to how others are suffering."

"I believe he understands more than most," Brock said. "I haven't spoken to Dani about the Major's recovery, but Sidney's told me some. They had quite a struggle with his health for years. He was depressed to the point of being suicidal at one point in his life. He had PTSD plus physical injuries that held him back from living a full life. But if you look at him now, he's a completely different man."

Words to live by. *A completely different man.* That was Brock too. Cole remembered seeing Brock in the hospital after his injuries and thinking how terrible his friend looked. It wasn't just physical—it was emotional and mental too. Now the buddy pushing him around this place was a whole new man all over again. That was Cole's goal in life—to be a whole new man because the old one sucked.

Chapter 6

S ANDRA WOKE THE next morning feeling more at peace
than she had for eons. For the first time in a long time
she hadn't woken up in tears. Weeks had gone by since
Cole's arrival, and he'd settled in well. The only recurring
problematic factor showing up in the team's weekly meetings
regarding Cole's progress came from his psychiatrist and his
therapist and dealt with his inability to open up. Which was
a shame as any psychological findings could benefit the
therapist's ability to help Cole deal with any false beliefs that
may be holding him back in reaching his goals. The psychiatrist was still looking for the root issues in Cole's life, which
his therapist would then help him deal with, but Cole
avoided the trauma of his IED explosion, even more earlier
events in his life, only wanting to face forward with no
resolution of past dramas. The psychiatrist was not giving up
and kept prodding each week.

As for Cole's therapist, Kimmy was happy to see Cole's
forward-facing mentality, yet Cole was unfocused as to his
second career. In one of the team meetings, Sandra had
asked if maybe Cole would respond better to an informal
conversation, like with her, and how he might feel pressured
with these recurring themes when seeing his psychiatrist and
his therapist. The two doctors conferred and agreed. Sandra
would pass on any further insights she discovered.

Except for the two mental blocks noted at several team meetings, Cole was making good overall progress, not overextending himself physically, yet following his doctor's orders, taking his medications as prescribed. Sandra and Cole were in a routine now, and that was a good thing for everyone. In a place like this, routine kept everything moving forward.

She was still hesitant around Cole, but a bond was forming, and that was the way she liked it. It was nice to become friends with these people when they were here. However, on a day like today, it was harder. Isaac would leave this morning. She was so happy for him, but still it would be tough because she probably would never see him again.

It happened that way most of the time. Patients talked about keeping in touch, but in her experience, it was rare— the odd email, maybe a thank-you card. But as people integrated back into their real, normal lives, the stages of their recovery faded into insignificance. Maybe it was supposed to be that way, but it left her without that sense of any long-term continuity of that friendship, and she was sad for that reason.

She waited at the front entrance. Isaac's cab ride was here, waiting for him to make the final walk out the front door. He would leave under his own steam, walking on his own two feet and carrying his own two bags. If there was ever a change, it was this man who had shown up in such bad shape. This was one of the biggest and most startling transformations she had witnessed.

She stood and watched as Isaac, who'd lost both legs, walked toward her, a massive grin on his face. He'd have been a hell of a football player with the size of his chest and shoulders. He had taken his injuries hard, but unlike so many others, he hadn't gotten depressed—he'd gotten even. He was the best he could be right now. He even walked normally. It would take a skilled medical professional to spot the shifts of his prosthetic limbs. Isaac was doing so well.

When he saw her, his grin widened. "I was hoping to see you before I left."

"I wouldn't let you go without saying goodbye," she said, and damn it if there weren't tears choking her throat.

He put down his bags, opened his arms and gave her a gentle hug.

That was the thing about Isaac. He was a giant physically, but his personality had been that of a teddy bear. They would miss him. She stepped back to wipe the tears from her face. "It was a delight working with you, and you will be missed."

He smiled. "Don't take it personally, but I hope I never come back."

She laughed. "And we hope we never see you as a patient here again."

"Don't worry. I'll stay in touch."

She smiled because she'd heard it all before. He said goodbye to several of the other residents, and then he walked out into the sunshine. His sister wanted to pick him up, but he had said no. He would start his new life the way he intended to go on—independent. As the taxi drove away, she turned toward the hallway, but she still wiped away her tears.

"You okay?" Cole asked as he appeared in front of her.

She stopped in her tracks. She smiled at him, maybe for the first time with a free, open, happy smile. "I'm sad and happy at the same time. Someone who was here for months and who had an incredibly difficult recovery just walked out of here carrying his own bags. He's flying out to California on his own. He'll make it."

Cole looked at her and then smiled. "I guess that's the ultimate joy for you."

"Joy and sadness. We're a part of the stage of their lives that they don't ever want to remember. So we all ..." She shrugged and took a deep breath. "In most cases we are forgotten." She continued past him and then froze. "Oh, my gosh. You're not in the wheelchair."

COLE LAUGHED. "YOU noticed, did you?" He kept his voice light and carefree. Inside, he was beaming because he was on crutches. He hadn't gone very far yet, but it made such a difference to be fully vertical and mobile. Besides, when he'd seen her walk past, he'd made a special effort to reach her, just so she would see him. So silly. Yet, he couldn't stop himself from thinking about her. She most likely didn't even notice him most days. He'd been a problem for her in the beginning, and now he was sure she was keeping her distance. She maintained a professional eye on him, but that was it.

The last couple weeks he had developed an interest in Sandra, but he knew that was foolish. Still, something about Brock and Sidney's relationship made Cole realize his physical form wouldn't necessarily stop him from finding somebody he liked. Only one person in this entire place made his heart race and his gaze stare at the doorway every time he heard footsteps in the hall. She came into his room two to three times a day, and although these were profession-al visits, he couldn't help but wish they were something more.

Immediately she frowned. "Are you sure you're not doing things too fast? I know you think you're getting that much better, faster …"

"I am getting better, faster. And yes, I do have permission to be on crutches. Although I can't go very far. This is my first run. I don't want to screw anything up and overstress other parts." He grinned at her. "But it's absolutely awesome to be on my feet again."

She beamed at him. "It's a huge mental shift that we see a lot here. I'm so happy you've reached that point."

He grabbed her hand, brought it to his lips. "So am I."

Sandra's expression was stunned, and a knot formed in Cole's stomach. *Play it off, dude.*

He winked at her and turned, then said, "Race you to the other end of the hall."

He had no idea what made him say that. He knew she stared after him with that surprised look. Escape was the only option. But when hobbling around on crutches for the first time, he wouldn't likely escape quickly. Maybe his challenge would give her an excuse to run away. Hell, that was what he wanted to do.

"Hold up," she called out. "No running."

He tossed her a disbelieving look, and the twist of his torso was just enough to throw his weight off-balance. He quickly stuck out one crutch to catch himself before he went down. At least he was still standing. But his back was screaming.

She gasped and raced to his side. "Are you okay?"

He closed his eyes and bowed his head. "I'm fine. Just doing too much." Then he heard the same damned echo in his head, all over again—*going too fast, going too far, going too soon.* Jesus, when would he ever learn? In his own embarrassment, he'd "run away," and he had done more damage than if he'd just casually walked off.

He gave her an embarrassed smile and took ownership. "That'll teach me." He nodded at his room one doorway down. "Good thing I'm almost there." He left her and made his way to his room where he sat on the bed and laid his crutches across the end. Using his arms, he shuffled up the bed and collapsed. He knew he hadn't hurt himself badly. But at the same time, it had been a jolt to his senses. A fall might've been good. It might've stopped him from trying something like that again. "What the hell was I even thinking?" he muttered.

He could sense her in the doorway. He willed her to disappear. The last thing he wanted was her pity, her sympathy or even her amusement, although that would be a hell of a lot better than the other two.

"I'm fine," he said, waving an arm at her to go away. "You don't have to worry."

"I'm not worried. I'm just a little concerned."

"There's hardly a difference." He rolled over to face the window. "I always like to make a fool of myself. It's a great way to meet girls." Only the words came out more sarcastic than he'd intended. He shook his head, but he didn't hear any retreating footsteps. Instead, she laughed.

Then he heard her soft voice from the doorway. "There are lots of ways to meet girls. Please don't hurt yourself as one of them. If you want coffee sometime, I'm certainly up for that."

Then all he heard was her footsteps, almost racing down the hall. He lay there on the bed with a slow, wide grin growing on his face. Hell, he'd fall to the floor anytime if it meant getting that response.

Chapter 7

WHAT HAD POSSESSED her to do something so foolish? Sandra raced to her office. She glanced at her watch, now a bit behind in her rounds. Seeing Isaac off had put her behind schedule, but that moment with Cole had set her back even further. On the other hand, she'd also seen something that tickled her pink. She had deliberately held back from getting too close to any of the patients over the years, but she could blame Dani for any shift in that now. Dani and Sidney. They both had relationships with men who they had met here.

That was both good and bad. Good in the sense that she was delighted for them, but bad as it also highlighted what those without a relationship were missing. She'd liked Cole right from the beginning, but when his condition had declined and he'd gone back to the hospital, she'd been so worried about his health that she'd pulled back, not wanting to hinder him in any way. Sure, he was back again and doing very well, but from what she could see, he still appeared to be headstrong and driven to do too much.

It wasn't that those were bad traits, but they had to be held in check. That he liked her was obvious, and it made her feel good because she really liked him too. However, she wasn't sure she could live with his headstrong-and-driven personality. She was slow and cautious. She was a taking-safe-steps-forward type of person, whereas he appeared to dive in and damn the consequences.

Maybe that was his military training. She imagined it took serious guts to throw himself out of planes and to scuba dive in rough waters and all the other activities she'd heard the men did. Her world was built on routine, on a strict regimen. It was built on safety. She helped people get better. Any mistake on her part—well, it could kill a patient. Of course, any mistake on his part could also kill him. She shook her head at the contrast ... and the similarities.

At her desk, she updated her computer records. Her tablet would sync automatically. Then she set out the medications to dispense.

One of the biggest problems in her professional interactions with the male patients at Hathaway House was the fact they often viewed the relationship between the people who they worked with and themselves in an unhealthy light. They put too much emphasis on the gratitude, or whatever you wanted to call it, that they felt toward the people who worked with them every day. Like they latched on to that person and didn't see them in a real light. She'd seen that happen a lot. Take Kenneth for example. Some patients—and staff—found it hard to separate a healthy relationship from that type of dependent relationship here. Being a friendly and helpful caregiver should never be taken as something else. Which was Kenneth's biggest flaw. She didn't see that same problem in Cole.

Yet, Sidney and Dani were lucky to have healthy relationships with Brock and Aaron, who were both stable and solid. The two couples seemed very much in love.

Sandra would like to find a healthy relationship like that for herself.

For the first time, she felt Cole may feel the same way. But what exactly? It wasn't something she was prepared to push. She was all about moving forward slowly and carefully. Whereas, she could already see he was the guy who jumped into things—maybe relationships too. She wouldn't go there too quickly.

Still, the look of embarrassment on his face when he'd almost fallen and his comment when he lay in bed—well, she'd seen a side to him she hadn't seen before. She wasn't sure that was a good thing because it endeared him to her that much more.

She quickly finished selecting her medications, picked up the tray and made her rounds. She went from patient to patient, dispensing pills. When she came to Cole's room, she knocked on the door. He was still lying down, facing the window.

"Cole?" she said. "It's me again."

He rolled to his back, looked at her and smiled. "I figured I'd chased you away."

She grinned. "I don't chase away that easy."

"Glad to hear it." He propped himself up on the bed, motioned her over, accepted his medication and reaching for his water bottle, threw the whole lot down at once. He handed her the empty paper cup and said, "I'll be happy when I'm off these."

She nodded. "You and many other people." As she went toward the door, she glanced back and said, "No ill effects from the crutches?"

He laughed. "No idea. I haven't gotten up again."

She glanced at her watch. "I'm going for coffee in about ten minutes, if you want to meet me in the dining room. I like to sit out on the deck where the sun is. If you make it, great. If not"—she shrugged—"no problem."

"*IF I MAKE it, great. If not, no problem*," he repeated. *Like hell.* This was his first chance to cement a small step here—so very necessary for the rest to follow. Sure, he was tired. But he wasn't completely done. He looked at the crutches, then at the wheelchair, and realized he might be better off in the wheelchair. Proving it was one thing—stupidity was another. He slowly lowered himself into the wheelchair and laid the crutches across the bed one at a time.

Settling himself into a better position, he placed his hands on the wheels and headed out the door. The hallway was empty, which was a good thing as his control of the wheelchair left a lot to be desired. He'd seen some guys do amazing things in theirs from climbing stairs to any number of other feats. They were all way beyond him. The trouble was, he also didn't *want* to be very good at maneuvering a wheelchair. This wasn't his life or permanent base.

This was his life *for now.* He felt better, more like his old self on the crutches, but he had to admit it was easier on his body to sit in the wheelchair.

It was early afternoon, which meant the dining area was quiet. He was thankful for that. It made it so much easier to get around when he didn't have to dodge people, even though there was plenty of room between the tables.

He was a little on the hungry side. He rolled up to the coffee bar and filled a cup. He studied the treats on offer and decided on a cinnamon bun, so famously delightful here. They appeared to be warm. He put one on a tray, along with his coffee, then picked up the tray and gingerly placed it in his lap. He reached over and grabbed a handful of paper napkins in case of accidental spills, then slowly turned the wheelchair and headed at what he would call a relaxed pace out to a table in the sunshine. To his surprise and satisfaction, he arrived without spilling anything. He grinned. Success was nice.

"That's a pretty happy smile on your face there, champ," Sandra said, coming around the table. She held a cup of coffee in one hand and a cinnamon bun in the other. She laughed. "Great minds think alike, huh?"

Still worried about dumping the coffee, Cole carefully transferred the tray to the table. Sandra moved a chair out of the way so he had room to wheel up against the table. He relaxed back in his chair.

"The whole way here, all I could think about was that damned cup. I was so sure I'd end up wearing it."

She grinned. "You wouldn't be the first."

He nodded. "That doesn't mean I want to be the last either."

"*Latest*," she corrected with a smile. "There will be many more. But take the successes as they come."

He removed the coffee cup and the cinnamon bun from the tray and set it off to one side. Something about trays made him think of hospitals. He hated them. He sat back and studied Sandra as she tucked into the pastry. She didn't take little delicate bites, but she ripped off part of the big coil in her fingers, and then she sat back and moaned. The joy on her face made him smile in anticipation, which had nothing to do with the cinnamon bun but more about the tightening in his groin, wanting to put that kind of smile on her face himself.

Dangerous thoughts, especially here. He gave his head a

shake and reached for his treat. She seemed to make it clear he was a patient and nothing more. And it was best things stayed that way. Right?

Pushing away those thoughts, he took his first bite of the cinnamon bun. "Wow, this is really good."

She nodded, her mouth too full to reply.

He grinned as he watched her slowly uncoil the entire cinnamon bun and eat it bite by bite while he took a chunk from the side like some wild animal. "I wonder if they've ever done any research on the way people eat cinnamon buns."

She glanced up, took one look at the way he ate his and said, "Yep, and you're eating it wrong." She flashed that grin at him again and peeled off another piece.

"I never really thought about it. I pick it up and bite."

"It's best if you unwrap it first. My favorite part is the very center."

"Right." His throat suddenly clogged as his thoughts became wayward once more, focusing on the best parts of her being in her center. He swallowed hard and turned to stare at the fields around them. "It's truly beautiful here."

"It's also incredibly rare. This is a green oasis in Texas."

He grinned and nodded. "Where are the dust bowls and the tumbleweeds?"

"Not for a few miles around here, that's for sure."

"Dani and her father could sell this property for millions."

Sandra shook her head. "Hopefully they won't. The center is doing a tremendous job helping people."

Keeping the conversation light and neutral, he asked her about her work. "How long have you been here?"

"Five years. And with any luck, I'll stay for another ten

to fifteen at least."

"What about marriage and family?"

She nodded. "Absolutely. But one doesn't preclude the other. I'd love to stay here, working, even if it's only part-time. I've seen a lot of my friends lose track of their careers and become very isolated once they have children, especially if they stop working full-time. It's hard at first, but once you get that work-life balance, it's nice to have an adult life and not days full of baby talk. Even if it's only for one or two days a week. We're close enough to Dallas that a lot of people here commute daily."

"Don't they all?" He glanced around and added, "It never occurred to me that staff quarters were available here."

She laughed. "They are, indeed. Not terribly luxurious but comfortable, and you get the advantages of the pool on the grounds and the food." She held up the last bite of cinnamon bun to emphasize her point. "There are an awful lot of pros and not too many cons about being here."

"I hadn't thought of it, but it's a great idea."

"A lot of the staff are married and have houses between here and Dallas. We also have a number of specialists who regularly make the trip from the big city too." She smiled. "I remember when a spinal surgeon from Dallas came to visit a friend of his, who'd opted to spend his recovery time here. The surgeon was dubious in the beginning, but he is a convert now. He sends us a lot of people. He also stops by to check on some of his patients occasionally. It's close enough for him to come in whenever he's a little worried."

Cole sat back. "That says an awful lot about the job that's being done here."

"Exactly." She glanced up and smiled. "Speaking of which, hello, Major."

The Major stepped around the table into Cole's view and held out his hand. "I'm Don Hathaway—or the Major as a lot of people call me—and of course, I'm Dani's father."

"Nice to meet you." Cole reached out and shook the man's hand, studying the cross between Santa Claus and Rip Van Winkle. Don wasn't quite as large as Santa, and Don didn't have the super long Rip Van Winkle beard, but the Major's contagious smile matched both images. "This is a hell of a place you've developed here."

"Thank you." The Major nodded, and Cole realized Don carried a small dog.

Sandra reached out and said, "Hello, Chickie."

There was the tiniest of yelps as the animal shifted in the Major's arms. Cole stared at the little critter, fascinated. "Is that a dog? Or maybe a rat? I'm not sure."

Chapter 8

S ANDRA GRINNED. CHICKIE was unique.

The Major laughed—big belly laughs that rolled across the open porch. "This is Chickie. He's a four-year-old Chihuahua cross. He has stunted growth, and he's physically deformed. But he's extremely well-loved by everyone. Here." With a sudden move, the Major handed Chickie to Cole.

Sandra watched as Cole held out his hands but had no idea what to do with the dog. He lifted him to eye level, clearly studying the huge brown eyes that stuck out of a very small head. Chickie's eyes held so much trust. Intelligence. And hope.

As if unable to resist, with a reaction she'd seen time and time again, Cole bent and nuzzled the little dog's head with his cheek. Chickie's little *yip, yip* was audible from where she sat. Cole cuddled the dog close against his chest. Chickie laid his jaw against Cole's shoulder and snuggled in.

"Chickie is a special family member here," Sandra said, her heart melting to see this guy take to Chickie—and Chickie take to him—so easily. "He's well-loved, and although he has lots of his own physical problems, he is a mascot of hope for everyone here."

Cole nodded, and Sandra could see the faintest shimmer of wetness in his eyes.

"We always make a point of introducing him to everybody, and we let everybody know he's on a special diet and can't be fed anything off the table," the Major said. "The last time that happened, he ended up with a bowel blockage, and he had surgery to help him with that."

Cole looked at Chickie and shook his head. "I promise I will not feed him."

"He obviously would like it if you do," Sandra said with a big grin. "Like all dogs. But he doesn't jump well, and although he walks, he is so darned small that most people end up carrying him around. Which, as you can see, suits him entirely."

Cole nodded and gently rubbed his chin back and forth against the dog's small head. "Does he live here?"

"Several of them do," Sandra said. "Chickie has a basket in the front reception area. Helga lives here too. She's a big Newfoundland with a prosthetic leg. She makes the rounds to every room here at some point in time. She has an uncanny nose for finding people who might need a canine hug. An assigned member of the kitchen staff makes sure meals are brought to the dogs twice a day and that they have water available when needed. Other than that, we give them access to the outdoors. They're all house-trained as much as they can be, but there might be the occasional accident," Sandra said calmly. "We understand when that happens. For animals and people alike."

She didn't know if Cole got the message. This place was all about acceptance. He needed to know that. Even when people made false starts, it was okay when they got up and moved forward again. She expected Cole had a lot more setbacks coming. It was the nature of life, and it was very much the nature of recovery.

"A dog called Racer was here for a while. He had wheels.

I haven't seen him in a few days. I should ask about him."

"Wheels, huh? I guess that makes sense." He glanced over at Sandra. "It would be nice to spend some time with Stan and the animals. I've always been a huge dog lover." He cuddled Chickie closer. "Something about their ability to love unconditionally ... and animals like this are so much smaller and yet so much more trusting. They can step in and comfort you when you're dealing with so much garbage," he said. "It's really special."

"That's one of the benefits here." She smiled. "In the beginning, a lot of people were concerned about the hygiene issues between animals and people. Infections are a problem anywhere, but the upstairs is sanitized on a regular basis. So is the downstairs, for that matter, because the animals are healing too. A lot of the animals, such as Racer, had to have surgery. This little guy had surgery as well, but that was a long time ago." She glanced at Chickie. "Are you okay with Chickie? Do you want him a bit longer, or do you want me to take him now?"

Instinctively, he wrapped his arms around the little guy to keep him close.

She smiled. "I wanted to make sure that he's comfortable here with you, and considering his delicate system that he doesn't need to go out."

"Right. Then I guess I should give him back." He gently picked up the little dog and kissed him on the top of his head before handing him to the Major. "If you don't mind, maybe I'll get a chance to visit with him later."

"Absolutely," the Major said. "If you don't see him around, go to the front desk. He could be sleeping in his bed there. He is in popular demand, but sometimes he is completely alone and looking for somebody to love too."

The Major scooped up Chickie and tucked him against his shoulder and headed back inside, into the dining hall.

Sandra turned toward Cole. "Two of our biggest icons in this place are the Major and Chickie."

Cole smiled. "I'm sure life would not be the same without having characters like those two in it."

COLE'S ARMS FELT empty without Chickie in them. He wanted to get a dog when he was in a better situation. He had had a small apartment in California, but his landlord had put his stuff in storage for him, rather than Cole continuing to pay the rent. He knew he probably wouldn't return to something like that anyway—one of those old buildings that didn't have an elevator. Right now, for all intents and purposes, he was homeless. That felt very strange. When he'd been living on base, he had housing. Then, for a while, he'd moved off base and had his own apartment.

Now he wasn't entitled to base living as he was no longer active in the military. He wouldn't ask to go back either. It wasn't his life anymore. No matter how much he wished things could have been different, this was his new reality, and he had to make decisions about his future. He'd been an IED man, but there was not a whole lot of work for bomb specialists in civilian life. With the physical requirements to be on a police force, he wasn't sure that was an option for him, now that he was physically disabled. He didn't see how any of his work history and SEALs experiences would help him in a second career.

That meant retraining. He had some funds socked away and could get government assistance, but he needed a goal to shoot for. It was also hard, if not almost impossible, to think about what his options were when he hadn't even healed yet, didn't know what his new physical abilities would be. Everything seemed so out of reach, and when he tried to reach out, he felt he was being left behind. Like with his much-older brothers when he was a kid.

Yet Cole *had* to move forward regardless, albeit slowly now, a little bit at a time, one step after the other. He couldn't start thinking long-term *yet*. Not until he was better, both physically and emotionally. He'd use Brock as a model. The man had been broken inside and outside for such a long time, but to see him now, well, he was just so different. Cole was so happy for his buddy, and he wanted that same success. He didn't know what Brock planned to do with his life now, but Cole was sure it would incorporate Sidney in some way.

Dallas wasn't very far away as Sandra had said. Lots of people lived there and commuted here. Hathaway House was probably only ten to fifteen minutes from the outskirts of the city limits and a half hour more from downtown.

He'd heard Dani's fiancé, Aaron, had applied and been accepted for veterinarian school, most likely with Stan's help, but that wasn't the life for Cole. He loved animals, but he certainly didn't want to be a veterinarian, dealing with sick and broken pets all his life. He had no idea what he did want to do, and that would be an issue—but not one for today.

He suddenly realized Sandra was still here, staring at him, a concerned frown on her face. He gave himself a mental shake. "I'm sorry. I'm sitting here, lost in my own worries, when I should be enjoying my time with you." He reached across the table and held out his hand. He was gratified when she reached across too.

"You're a very special woman. I don't know how you can handle all of us broken people as easily and as well as you do."

She smiled. But the smile didn't reach her eyes.

"I'm fine," he said gently. "I've got a lot of things going on inside that I have to realign to my new world."

She nodded. "How true. We see that a lot. Some people had lives before the military. Some people have lives they can go home to with skills they learned from the military, and other people are starting all over again."

He smiled wryly. "Put me in the starting-all-over-again category."

"But your counselor will give you aptitude tests and career counseling and things like that," she said. "You'll still have to make some decisions, but you may discover several options are available to you."

She smiled again, and this time her smile did reach her eyes.

He stared at her long fingers, her perfectly trimmed nails. She had the gentle, soft fingers of a nurse's hand. He reached his other hand across the table, laying it beside hers, and opened his palm with its large square calluses. The difference was instantly obvious.

"Even before I went into the military, I was more of a physical worker. Not like Brock, who was a roofer, doing any construction job he got his hands on. I was always into landscape, gardening." He smiled. "At one point, I thought I would have my own company. I like to build small walls, fences and ponds." He shook his head. "That was a long time ago."

"Maybe it's something you could go back to. There is something very nurturing and healing about working in gardens," she replied, making a mental note to share this with Kimmy.

"I'm sure there are at least a hundred, if not a thousand, landscaping companies in Dallas alone."

"That doesn't mean there isn't room for another one. Or that you couldn't work for one of them if you wanted to."

"But it's physical work," he reminded her. "That makes it not a great option."

She settled back thoughtfully, her fingers drumming on the table beside his. "Maybe," she said slowly. "But that doesn't mean you can't hire people. If you're the boss, you won't be doing a ton of the physical labor anyway. Physically, you *can* get back a lot of your strength. Look at Brock."

Cole nodded. "Brock is my idol right now," he said with a smile. "The fact is, he's also a good guy."

"Has he lined up his future career?"

"I'm not sure. We haven't spoken about that. But he was hell on computers before. So I imagine his job prospects are a bit better than mine."

"Maybe. But there is room in the world for everybody. Everybody has options. Even you." She stood and smiled. "As nice as it is to sit here and visit, I need to get back to work." She took several steps away and then turned. "I imagine you have something you're supposed to do now or someplace else you're supposed to be."

He frowned at her and then saw what time it was. "Oh, crap. You are so right." In fact, he was already late.

Chapter 9

T HE NEXT FEW days followed a gentle and routine pattern for Cole. Sandra stopped in to say hi during her rounds. They got coffee together midmorning, and she saw him again in the evening. She knew he didn't see the same improvement she did. Then again, she was watching for it. It could take weeks before that sudden, magical moment happened, where the patient saw the improvement.

But day by day, taking it slow and steady, Cole got squared away and built up some strength. He was working a lot with Shane in the morning and then swimming in the afternoon with Brock. She was happy for Cole. His mood had shifted as well. A team meeting on his progress was scheduled for this afternoon. She'd be interested to hear what the others had to say about him. A couple people had commented on the fact that she was spending a fair amount of time with him, but so far, she had tossed that off as a joke. She knew it was noticeable, but she hadn't made up her mind what to do about it.

Dani had not said anything to Sandra about relationships not being allowed. Dani was with Aaron after all.

Anyway, Sandra didn't think that was on Dani's agenda. No, it was more about Sandra and what she would do for herself. She wanted to be sure her job remained secure. And she was uncertain that she wanted to get involved with somebody who would just turn around and leave. She planned to stay here, and if Cole wasn't staying local, then that wouldn't work long term.

She walked into the meeting room, tablet in hand, and took her seat. When everybody was there, the meeting began with a number of patients to review. They went through several case folders without any disagreement. Then they came to Cole.

She brought up Cole's folder on her tablet, and Shane started.

"He's come a long way in these last few weeks. One thing I would say is that he seems to be holding back. I think his initial arrival and doing too much has stopped him from applying himself now. He's afraid to set himself back any further."

Cole's therapist Kimmy nodded. "He won't open up about some issues as well. Not that we need to know every deep, dark secret he has, but we don't want anything that adds stress or has a negative impact on his healing."

The discussion carried on around the table.

"Is he making any friends here?" one of the psychiatrists asked.

After a moment of silence, everybody turned to look at Sandra.

She flushed. "I'm friendly with him, yes, but I'm hoping he's making new friends with other people too." Several of them looked at their tablets, and she wondered what was going on. "Do you think that, because we're friends, he's not joining in with other people?"

"I wondered if that was an issue with him," Shane said. "He is, however, friendly with Brock. Because he has the two of you as his cornerstones, quite possibly he is keeping himself apart from the others. We do see that. Until the patient settles in, it's hard for them to integrate."

"Is that an issue with Cole?" Sandra asked bluntly. The last thing she wanted was for anybody to be concerned about this and not bring it up, then it come back to bite her later.

There was silence for a moment. Then Shane spoke again. "I think integrating would help. I guess I'm a little more concerned that he's not putting in his full efforts. It's like he's found his comfort zone, and he's stuck there."

"Oh." Sandra studied Shane. "Do you think that's because of a friendship?" She frowned. "I'm not sure how that would be."

"No." He shook his head. "I shouldn't have linked those two together. I don't think they are related. When he first got here, he pushed himself too hard and too fast, and he had a natural relapse. But when he arrived the second time, it was as if he was scared to try. At the same time, he could see Brock, and he wanted what Brock had." He held up a hand to forestall Sandra's question. "I don't mean that as Cole wanting a relationship. I mean how Cole wants Brock's very much improved level of physical fitness."

She settled back, realizing Shane wasn't saying anything derogatory. He was just laying out the facts as he saw them.

Speaking slowly, Shane continued. "But at the same time, there is almost a disconnect. Because he tried once and hurt himself, he is scared to give that full effort again. So I can see some discouragement in him right now. It's like he's got an issue of *before versus now*. If he tries too hard, he'll push himself back. If he doesn't try enough, he's not reaching his goal. Brock's the goal. Cole doesn't see how to get from where he is to where he wants to be."

"I can see that," Sandra said. She glanced around the

room at everybody else. "Anybody else have something to add?"

"It's all about fear," one psychiatrist said bluntly. "He's afraid he will fail. He's afraid he'll set himself back. He's afraid he'll never reach Brock's state. He's afraid he'll always be *half-as-good*. He was a SEAL. Brock was a SEAL. They are incredibly competitive, but there they were equals. Cole doesn't see himself as Brock's equal right now. He's behind the curve and is afraid he'll never catch up."

A flash of sympathy tugged at Sandra's heart, but she knew sympathy would not be helpful. "What's the answer?"

The psychiatrist faced her and smiled. "What did you do?"

She frowned at him. "I didn't do anything."

He grinned. "After you found out that Cole had tossed his medicines, how did you react and get back on track?"

She stared at him, not happy being put in the hot seat for her own behavior. But these meetings were all about making helpful and constructive progress moving forward, so she didn't have a lot of choice but to answer.

"I locked down and became more paranoid. I watched all the patients, ensuring they took all their medications, not just one. I still do that," she confessed. "It grabs a hold of you, and you're scared of making a mistake. The same as Cole must feel."

"So how do we help him?"

Maybe an answer to that question would be of help to her too. The more she thought about it, the more she realized she had eased back already on her paranoia. Why? Because of Cole's change in attitude.

"We give him time to let him work through the issues and be there for him," she said quietly. "We learn to trust him as he must learn to trust us."

COLE LOOKED UP as Brock sat beside him. Cole was constantly amazed at how good his buddy looked.

"How you doing, Cole?" Brock put his coffee on their table, sitting in the shade out of the hot sun. "How's the therapy work going?"

Cole winced. "Alternately painful and not bad."

Brock laughed. With a commiserating nod he said, "I think everybody here can relate to that. When you give it your all, it hurts like absolute crap the next day. But slowly, day by day, and with continued hard work, you can see the results."

Cole dropped his gaze to his coffee cup. He nodded as if he understood. The trouble was he understood something different.

"What's the matter?" Brock asked.

Cole shrugged and shifted in his seat. He stared out at the large open area. "I guess I haven't seen the progress I wanted to see."

"Keep at it. You'll get there."

"I don't think so in this case," Cole said quietly. "I like that you're here. Fact is, I want the healing results you have, but I'm just not getting them."

"How long have you been here now? Four weeks?"

Cole nodded. "Give or take a few days."

"And your first week was all about a slow start, right?"

Again Cole nodded. "But after that it's been steady."

"Absolutely. If you look back to your condition when you initially arrived, versus where you are today, you'd see the change for yourself. Instead, you're comparing yourself to me, and that's not good. I have been here working my ass off for months now. I'm almost free and clear," Brock said, "but not quite."

Cole felt a rush of pride for his friend. "Now that would be awesome." He smiled at Brock. "Did you do anything special? Was there any one thing you can think of that helped your recovery?"

Brock shook his head. "I don't know about *one* thing specifically, but I can list several. One was getting Sidney as my therapist because she took my motivation, which was nil, and supercharged it to a hundred percent. Then having Sidney come into my life in a personal way definitely helped."

"Well, that's not my case obviously." Cole slouched back in his chair.

"If she was your therapist, would you be motivated to do the work you need to do?" Brock lifted his cup and took a sip of his coffee. "Or are you scared of a relapse?"

Cole looked up and let out a slow breath. "Before the relapse, I was absolutely determined to get the exact same results as you. I would beat your time. I would kick your ass. I would make sure I owned this place," he said. "I wanted my body back in the biggest way." He picked up a spoon and stirred his black coffee, studying the swirling pattern in the cup. Then he continued in a low voice. "When I came back the second time, I was terrified. They warned me about not doing too much." He sighed. "Now I feel like I'm lost in the middle ground. I'm scared to give it my all because that setback scared the crap out of me."

"Understandable. It was rough on you at the time. Hell, it was pretty rough on me too." Brock smiled. "I was devastated when I heard you'd been taken back to the hospital."

"You and me both." Cole chuckled wryly. "From where I was, when I first returned here, to where I am today is a huge improvement, but it still seems like I am so damned far away. It's there within my grasp, but it's not. I can almost reach out and touch it." Cole grabbed Brock's arm. "I can see it in you. You made something magical happen. I'm looking for that same thing."

Brock turned his arm over so he could grab Cole's forearm. "But you weren't here to see my first three months as I struggled to get to where I am today. Plus, you don't see how you're actually making your own miracle happen right now. Because you're in the middle of the process, you can't see it yet. Remember when I was terrified of failing BUD/s training?"

Cole nodded. "It was easy to spot the fear because I felt the same damned thing."

"But we made it. We gave it our all, and we made it. What you must do is make that adjustment and understand, even if you give it your all right now, give everything Shane asks of you, you won't have a relapse. You could have a day where you feel like shit and think you can't do any more, but people like us, we can't say no." He stared into Cole's eyes. "We have to go all-in."

Cole smiled at him. "That was our motto, wasn't it? And so true. When we do something, we go all-in." He could feel something stirring inside him, the power that drove his desire to do better. It was that incredible competitiveness to do his best. "That's what I needed to hear."

Brock squeezed his buddy's arm and released him. "The other thing to remember is, when we were in BUD/s training, in many ways it was all about fighting the demons within yourself to find that best within you, so you could make it through the training. We did it as a team. We were together. We helped each other. We made it. There were days all of us were in tears, when all of us were broken, but *always* one of us wasn't as bad as the others, and that's what held us together. That's what pulled us up so we all made it."

"You're right. That's exactly it."

Brock nodded in agreement. "Before, when I was broken, I was at the lowest I could be. Now it's your turn to be down, and it's my turn to help you get back up."

"Too bad Denton isn't here."

Brock grinned. "That's something I wanted to talk to you about. I heard from Dent today. Dani called to tell him how things are looking good, and she hopes to have good news for him soon. It may be another three weeks until he knows for sure, but for however long I'm here, it'll be good to have the three of us together again, like old times."

"Good? Man, that is freaking awesome." That was the final clincher Cole needed to ignite the burning fire inside—it went from glowing coals to flames instantly. "You know he'll require a little help when he gets here, right?"

Brock nodded slowly. "That can be your job, dude. Like I'm here to help you, you can be here to help him. He'll see me and think that's too high a level to achieve. It'll be up to you to show him how very doable it is."

Feeling like Brock's words had rooted themselves somehow on the inside, Cole sat back in his chair, filled with determination. "Now *that* I can do."

Chapter 10

S ANDRA REMEMBERED THE conversation from the team
meeting many times over the next few days. In a way it
was unfinished, incomplete. She disagreed that her friendship with Cole could be detrimental to his progress. That
was like saying, hugging and petting the sick animals
downstairs would hinder the patients' recovery upstairs. She
wasn't Cole's therapist, and she wasn't a psychiatrist, but she
was a nurse, and he was one of her patients who she looked
after and kept an eye on.

But now that Cole was in much better physical shape,
her role was becoming redundant. She barely stepped inside
his room now as he was off most of his meds. When she did
go to his room, it was as a friend, and friendship should add
to any relationship. It shouldn't take away from it.

Of course, she'd already seen the beneficial results of a
relationship in Dani and Aaron, and in Sidney and Brock.
Even Cole's relationship with Brock. Sandra knew that had a
much bigger impact on Cole than his relationship with her.
Maybe it was supposed to be like that. If you stayed secluded
and didn't have to deal with all these issues, you also didn't
grow as a person. Even though the growing part could be
painful, there was so much joy afterward when you looked
back at how far you'd come.

Nobody at that meeting had suggested she step away

from the relationship. As she and Cole were only friends, she didn't feel she needed to. But a part of her worried all the same.

It was Friday afternoon, and she had a whole weekend off. She'd head to town tomorrow to do some shopping. She grabbed her tablet and a coffee and walked to the pool area. One of the advantages of her apartment was how close to the pool she lived. She sat in the sunshine, out of the way of the splashes, and brought up the list of things she had to do. When she heard her name, she glanced at the pool to see Cole swimming toward her side. She smiled. "You swim like a seal."

He gave a startled laugh. "I absolutely do." He hefted himself onto the side of the pool and sat there, the water dripping off him. She smiled, appreciating how much his body had grown and changed. He was no longer the same broken man. He wasn't completely fixed, but she could see the progress. She wondered if he could.

"What are you working on?" he asked.

"A shopping list of things I'll get in town tomorrow."

"Oh."

She glanced at him. "We do get weekends off, and this is mine." She shrugged. "We're on split shifts, so when I get a couple days off together, I'm happy to go to town."

He nodded. "Sounds like fun."

"You're welcome to come." She tossed off the invitation casually and then added, "But beware, I have a lot of shops to visit on my list."

He shook his head and said, "Not exactly my deal."

She grinned. "I don't know too many men who like to shop."

"I do if I need something," he said. "I'm not much on

window shopping."

"There are no windows on my list," she joked. "Do you need anything while I'm out?" She studied his face as he contemplated the question. Then he shook his head.

"In a couple weeks, I might enjoy a trip to town," he said. "But too many stops may be hard on me at this point, so I don't want to risk it."

"Still worried about doing too much?"

He shook his head, water droplets flying everywhere. A few of them landed on her legs, making her laugh and shift back a bit. "I'll take that as a no."

He grinned up at her. "Not worried about it. I just don't want to do anything that'll set me back. I know how hard it was to get here." He opened his arms and said, "And I'm a work in progress. I also know how hard it was mentally and emotionally with the initial setback." He shook his head. "I'll do a lot to avoid that."

"Very good thinking on your part," she admitted. "Make sure you're not holding yourself back from further progress out of fear."

He glanced at her. "Is that something you have dealt with before?"

She nodded. "I think we all have. Fear is a killer for so many of us."

"Fear is something I had to deal with throughout my training and when I went on missions," he said. "I can't say it's something I expected to feel during rehab. But it was one of the biggest stumbling blocks in the beginning. I wanted to do so well. I wanted to be a success story and was so afraid that, instead, I would be one of the worst-case scenarios." He flashed a tentative grin at her. "But slowly, step by step, as I see my own improvements, the fear abates, and in its place, I find self-confidence."

"As long as the self-confidence is in check, then everything's moving the way it should be."

He grinned at that. "Isn't that the truth? Overconfidence can be just as devastating as fear."

"It's all about balance," she said. She got up and walked to the edge of the pool, watching the blue water splashing up at the edges. "This pool is a genius idea."

"It is. I feel strong and vibrant in the water. The minute I get out, it's not the same feeling at all."

"I'm not a very good swimmer," she confessed. "I keep meaning to learn, but ..." She let her voice trail off.

"If that's something you would like to do," he said, "while I'm here, I can certainly teach you."

She glanced at him in surprise. "Really?"

He nodded. "I wasn't kidding when I said I was a SEAL. Water and I are best buddies." Then he rolled off the side into the water and did a series of laps, where he propelled his body up onto the surface and then let it flop back in again.

When he broke the surface, she was still smiling. "Okay, now that was very seal-like," she said. "I don't want to do that. Maybe the front crawl and the breaststroke."

"My daily schedule is done. I had my last therapy session, and it's like four o'clock. Go change and come back," he said. "We can do a quick lesson right now. Then you can practice any time after work."

She hesitated.

A teasing grin crept over his face. "Unless you're scared."

After their earlier conversation about fear, she glared at him. "That might have worked in high school, but it won't work on me now."

"Maybe, but it's also on your bucket list," he said.

"Knocking something off your list and learning a life-saving skill at the same time, that's well worth doing."

She studied the cool, refreshing-looking water and realized how much she'd always wanted to beat that demon. But she wasn't sure he was the right teacher.

"I don't know if I'm scared of the water or if I just don't know how to swim well enough," she confessed. "I've tried to swim in the past, but I never did it successfully."

"Go get changed," he ordered. "Then come back, and we'll find out. Come on. Don't make a big thing of this. Get into the water, and we'll sort it out."

She gave him a suspicious glance but then saw he was being sincere, so she nodded and turned and walked to her apartment. Once there, she changed into her bathing suit and grabbed a beach wrap and a towel and then walked back out. He was doing laps along the right-hand side of the pool. She walked to the shallow end and dropped her wrap and towel on a chair, feeling very self-conscious. She quickly slipped into the water.

As soon as she stood in waist-deep water, he appeared in front of her.

"Perfect," he said. "Now let's see how much you do know, and we'll go from there."

An hour of much fun and laughter followed as he taught her to float, something she still struggled with, and then he showed her the simple front crawl technique. She hated putting her face underwater and quickly realized that was one of her biggest hurdles. Then he switched to the breast-stroke. With her head out of the water, she had more confidence she could stay above water and yet still get from one end of the pool to the other. She managed six laps before her arms and legs felt shaky. She shook her head. "I had no idea I was so out of shape."

"It's not that you're out of shape, but you're pulling on muscles you don't normally use—and dealing with fear," he said quietly. "Both of those things stress you out more than anything."

She glanced at him and said, "I guess you know something about that."

He nodded. "More than I would like. Now let's go again. This time, do the front crawl again, and you can keep your head to the side so you can still see, but you will be getting one step closer to proper form."

The problem with that was she kept thinking. However, after she had made it to the other end of the pool and back again, she was improving slowly. When they finished that set, she pulled herself up to sit on the side of the pool.

"Now," he said, "you should practice every day if you can. If not, at least every second day for a few days. Then I'll come back, and we'll work on fine-tuning your technique. Once you get those down, it's all about practice and endurance. The more you do, the easier it becomes."

Feeling delighted with her progress, she dropped back into the water, threw her arms around his neck, and kissed him on the cheek. He hugged her close.

"I'm happy to give back," he said quietly. "Everybody here has treated me incredibly well."

She pulled away slightly and smiled. "It's easy to treat you well. You're a very special guy."

HE WOULD HAVE been happy to be more than just company for her—he wanted to be close to her. To build that bond and strengthen that little something they had into something so much more meaningful.

But if she thought he was a special guy, well, he wouldn't argue with her. If he could get another kiss as well, he wouldn't argue with that either. But neither would he put her in the same position Sidney had been in. No make-out sessions in the pool. He swam back slightly and whispered, "Last thing I want to do is get you into trouble, like Sidney."

Sandra wrinkled up her face and floated backward. "Good point." She shook her head. Then nodded to the side.

He turned and caught sight of Kenneth, another patient, and wondered how much he had seen, overheard.

She continued. "It's a sad world when somebody can't give a kiss of gratitude without certain people taking it the wrong way." She dove underwater.

He frowned. A kiss of gratitude? That was so not what he wanted. When she broke the surface again, he glanced around to make sure nobody was listening and said, "If this was a different place and time, I would show you a real kiss."

She threw him a startled look, and as if realizing what he meant, rich color rolled up her face. She dove underwater again.

Cole didn't blame her. He felt a bit antsy himself now. He probably shouldn't have said what he did. It was like stating his intentions. Putting the cart before the horse once again, pushing instead of pulling back. He sank underwater, pissed at himself for having taken such a step. He didn't want to scare her off.

He didn't want to make her nervous around him. He had meant his comment to be gentle, teasing and seductive. Instead, it had come off hard and critical and a little bit angry. Mind you, that was partly because of her comment about gratitude. He swam to the side and pulled himself up where he could sit on the edge of the pool. He glanced around, wondering how far he would have to go to get to his crutches.

Only somebody had moved them. Instantly, fear struck him inside. He didn't have his wheelchair here, his backup, for when he was tired. But without a wheelchair or his crutches, getting anywhere would be a lot harder. Sure, he could manage a few hops but only a few. He stared at his missing lower leg. He hadn't brought any of the prosthetics with him either. He was scheduled to get refitted for one Monday afternoon. Provided the stump was stable, free of infection and strong enough. He'd had a ton of trouble with that.

He glanced around, but he couldn't see anybody else nearby. His crutches now leaned against the changing room wall. Why the hell would somebody do that? Normally he was easygoing and laid-back about his property. He would lend stuff out and not be bothered if people were a little late returning things. But he had to admit he had struggled lately over having his own possessions in a specific spot. Moving his crutches though, well, that was just mean. He swiveled around and used the handles on the ladder to pull himself upright.

Of course water was everywhere—a hazard for those with two legs as well—which was one of the reasons the crutches had solid rubber bottoms. He could hop on one foot, but his crutches were probably twenty feet away. He couldn't afford to fall—that would be a failure. Yet, he also wanted to do this on his own, for even asking for help would be a draw in his mind, not an outright win. He wanted a success here.

With that thought uppermost, even knowing he would look ridiculous, he bent so his hands touched the ground and did a half-leapfrog action to his crutches. Not the debonair masculine can-do look he was going for.

With the crutches back in his hands, he headed to the changing room. The last thing he wanted to see was the look on her face. For sure, he wouldn't have minded getting his hands on the asshole who had moved his crutches. Once inside, he sat on one of the big wooden benches. He leaned back and closed his eyes. Every time he thought he was moving ahead, he hit something that sent him reeling backward. Nothing quite like the reality of not being able to walk from the pool to the changing room without looking like an idiot to bring a guy down a peg or two.

She would be so much better off with someone else. Someone whole. Someone who wouldn't embarrass her with the basic functions of life.

Chapter 11

S ANDRA BROKE THROUGH the water, happy to see Kenneth nowhere in sight and in time to see Cole making his way to his crutches in a rather unique manner. Why were they so far away? She knew some guys laid them literally alongside the edge of the pool, wanting the security of their tools near at hand. Still others deliberately placed things farther away to make it more difficult for themselves, pushing their own limits. She didn't think Cole would've done that, but she still didn't know him that well. She knew from their weekly team meetings Cole had yet to open up with his psychiatrist or with his therapist either. And it was their job to get him to talk about his issues, so she shouldn't feel shunned.

But she did.

When he didn't say goodbye to her or even wave at her in the pool but headed straight into the changing room, she wondered if he was upset with her.

She had kissed him impulsively. She was happy with her own progress with swimming and pleased he'd taken the time to teach her some basics. Instead, he'd seemed discomfited and afraid they might be seen. That she might get in trouble. And what about his comment afterward? Did he truly want to show her a real kiss, or was he teasing her again?

Out of sorts herself, she climbed from the pool and grabbed her cover-up and towel and headed to her own apartment. No point in asking Cole if he needed a hand. At this moment, chances were he'd just snap at her.

One thing she had learned a long time ago—pride was a highly motivating factor for a lot of men. She'd do nothing to take that away from them. Especially Cole. He'd had several setbacks already. She refused to make that worse.

Showered and changed, she walked upstairs to the dining hall, thinking about grabbing a late dinner before the buffet closed for the night, and then maybe spending some time outside. A few of the staff rode a couple horses here, and she hadn't gone for a ride in a long time. She wondered who might want to ride with her. It was not just about the safety of not going alone. Although she was a good rider, it was much nicer to go with someone.

The dining room was mostly empty, and the food was running out, but she still had some selection. She smiled to see the hot pasta and vegetables. She loved the food here. Because they offered such a wide variety, she could pick and eat as healthily as she wanted to. She grabbed a large salad and asked Dennis to chop up a chicken breast with some shaved Parmesan cheese. She chose a table outside in the sun and enjoyed her chicken Caesar salad.

Returning her dishes to the appropriate rack, she picked up a granola bar and an apple on her way out. Dani was probably still in her office. Sandra headed down the hallway, making a short detour to pass by Cole's room. The door was shut, and she wasn't exactly sure what that meant. She'd been in there many times, and she couldn't ever remember seeing the door closed. However, if he was having a private conversation with a doctor or someone, it made sense.

At Dani's office, Sandra was happy to see her friend still at her desk. Dani was buried in work, not ready to shut down for the day. "Hey, Dani." Sandra gave a sharp rap on the doorframe and walked inside. She shook her head at the stack of files on Dani's desk. "Maybe it's time you got an assistant."

Dani tossed down her pen and chuckled. "If I take on an assistant, it's one less therapist or one less nurse or person for the kitchen or for housekeeping." She smiled. "The budget only goes so far."

"I get that. How do you feel about going for a horseback ride?" she asked. "The walls are closing in on me today."

Dani's eyebrows rose in surprise. She glanced around at the paperwork, then checked her schedule on her computer. "You know what? Hell, yes. I've got no more meetings today, so give me a second to shut down my system and to put away a few files."

Happy to have company for her ride, Sandra sat in Dani's visitor's chair and waited. When Dani was done, the two women headed out.

"I've already eaten. Do you need anything first?" Sandra asked.

Dani shook her head. "I had a late lunch. And now a horseback ride sounds like the perfect medicine." She led the way to the stables attached to the veterinary clinic, and before long, she had Midnight saddled. She glanced over at Sandra. "Who do you want to ride?"

"I'll take Rose." The dapple was a favorite of hers. She was always easy to catch, making it a short job to get a saddle on and get out. Dani rode Western, whereas Sandra rode English. Neither horse seemed to mind whichever they did. Midnight was Dani's, however, and she was the only one who rode him.

Within minutes, the two women were in the pasture and loping along the acres of long grass, heading for the open fields in the distance. They made for the gate and soon were outside the main grounds, in the freedom of the world beyond Hathaway House.

Sandra lifted her face to the sun. "I so needed this today."

"Tough day?" Dani asked sympathetically.

"Not really. I've had much worse days."

"Is it Cole?"

Startled, Sandra looked over at her friend. "Cole?"

Dani shot her friend a knowing look. "I've seen the building attraction. The smiles, the touches, the extra glances. You care. He cares. It's lovely to see."

Sandra let her breath out in a heavy exhalation. "Is it? Sometimes I think we might get somewhere, and then it's like right back to square one."

"I think that's standard for all the men here." Dani smiled. "I wasn't sure about Aaron for a long time."

"But you are now?"

Dani grinned. "Definitely. We don't select an easy path when we choose one of the men from Hathaway House. They come here for a reason, and we aren't it."

"True enough." Sandra thought about that. "They also come with a lot more emotional baggage. It's not as if we've picked somebody up off the street or that we met at a friend's."

"I don't agree with that," Dani said. "I think that, in those cases, the emotional baggage is hidden. With the men here, it's easier to see what their baggage is. At least the initial layer of it. Sometimes they have deeper issues, where you have to ferret out what's wrong and why. It can be anything from survivor's guilt to feeling like they caused or brought on the accident themselves. Many of them suffer from PTSD." She shrugged.

"The thing with the men here is," Dani continued, "with so much going on, sometimes it's hard to figure out the core problems. Our military patients have extra problems, over and above what a lot of civilians have, but we deal with them. It gets brought up in the discussions in group therapy, and they work through them. Often they find that once they start working through one problem, other problems pop up because so much of it's connected. Before I started working here, I had never thought about that link. I finally learned that, even with my own problems, they could translate into dealing with other issues."

Sandra nodded. "It makes a lot of sense. I guess that's one of the extra benefits here. Once people are in therapy, it's hard to confine healing to a specific area."

"I think it's actually impossible," Dani said. "Yet, when you meet all these other apparently healthy normal males in the rest of the world, so few are dealing with their issues. They've shoved them all inside, and they think they're fine."

"Even if they're not."

Sandra thought back to some of the other relationships she knew about, such as Dani's last one before Aaron, where her ex had beaten the crap out of her. Sandra had never faced anything like that. Her last relationship had broken down because her boyfriend spent all his free time on video games. What was the point of a relationship if he didn't spend time with her? But he wasn't even interested in addressing that question. When they'd broken things off, she'd been relieved. "And yet Cole is something else." Sandra flushed when she realized she'd spoken aloud.

"You care about him, don't you?" Dani asked.

"I do. I just don't know how much." She gave her friend a small smile. "He dominates my thoughts from morning until night though."

"That's a lovely start."

COLE WATCHED FROM the deck as the two women rode off in the distance. Both were so natural and comfortable on the horses that they were a joy to watch. Both were whole, healthy and happy. His hands fisted as he stared at them. They were the opposite of what he was.

He was damaged and conflicted, and although he'd been improving mood-wise every day, right now he felt like he was back at the beginning. He should walk away from being friends with Sandra. *No*, from attempting to be more than friends.

He really liked her. But she deserved better than him.

Someone bumped into him, hard. Cole was still getting used to his prosthetic limb but remained standing, then glared at the guy—no crutches, no wheelchair, all his limbs intact.

"Dani's taken, and Sandra's mine. Stop staring at my girl."

Before Cole had decided how to best handle this situation—without getting kicked out of Hathaway House—Shane strode over, and the asshole left.

"You okay?" Shane asked, his phone to his ear.

Cole just nodded, watching the lunatic scurry off. From Shane's end of the conversation, Cole heard this guy was infatuated with Sandra. Why hadn't she told him? Cole would have handled this creep for her.

"Sounds perfect. I'll corral him while we wait for the police to arrive. Be good to have him gone."

So the guy was a problem, Cole thought. At least Hathaway House had procedures in place for this sort of thing. *At least they were taking care of it now. Should lighten up things for Sandra and the others.*

"Sorry, Cole. He'll be gone soon and won't bother you or anyone else anymore."

Cole knew Sandra and the other medical personnel here couldn't share patient information with another patient, but Cole got the gist of it. And that guy had looked normal. *Whole.* When he wasn't pushing Cole around or spouting lies.

But looks could be deceiving. And just because some guy hadn't lost a body part didn't mean he was healthy. *Hmm.*

Cole glanced around the dining area. The same and other related thoughts were probably running through the minds of every man and woman who were patients here. How did they reconcile their current selves to *who* they used to be, and how did they make peace with that, when they had wives and husbands and children?

Did they think they should walk away? Or did they feel loved enough, safe and secure enough in the relationship to stay and work through the multiple future obstacles in order to come to peace with their physical disabilities?

In theory, absolutely nothing should keep him and Sandra apart. They were both adults. Relationships were allowed here. Even relationships between patients and staff as evidenced by several of the relationships he'd already seen. Was *he* keeping them apart?

Not to mention, he didn't know if she was truly interested. Not after her "gratitude" kiss. Self-doubt crippled him. She was special to him, but here in this place, he was one of many to her. He wanted to be strong, to be the best, and to show her that he was still who he'd been before he got injured. Not that she knew that version of him. Yet, he'd been proud of that Cole. This Cole was beset by doubts and insecurities. His self-confidence was at an all-time low.

How could she love that? Surely she wanted a man to walk beside her, not someone she had to bolster all the time. Every time he tried to stand up and prove he was different, he was unique, he was better, something happened, and he took a step back.

Then he thought about Sandra's stalker patient with all his disabilities hidden inside. Cole looked down the hallway where the guy had disappeared. Cole's subconscious now lectured him: *Just be yourself. Stop worrying about it. If it's meant to be, it will be. Enjoy who she is. Don't look for more. Focus on your healing, not on a relationship. You're here for one reason—make that reason count. You'll never get another chance at it.*

All of that was true. At the same time, he had found something he wanted more than that.

He could thank the crazy guy for this revelation.

Cole didn't want one or the other, he wanted both. He wanted to be healed, strong, fit and ready to take on the world again—even if from a damaged physical perspective—and he wanted her at his side. *That was asking for a lot.*

Still, he argued with himself. *Why not? Why not reach for what I really want?*

That settled, his brain focused on more practical matters. How would he take care of himself and someone else in the future? He had no job, no decent prospects of a good job, no house. He had his bank account from his years in the military and a pension—it was small, but at least it was something.

How the hell was he to train for a new career? During the military, the team had teased Brock for all his computer geekiness. But now, with Cole's lack of education and lack of training for the real world, he had to wonder if maybe Brock hadn't had the better deal after all.

Still, there was lots Cole *could* do. But what did he *want* to do? He could go for some retraining, but no way would he attend a university for four years. That was not on the agenda. He wasn't sure he could handle a lesser degree or the two years required to get an apprenticeship or some other kind of heavy-duty training.

The money being what it was, along with the time and effort required, he didn't think he was up for extensive long-term training. So, what *could* he do with a minimum of training, and even better, if that training was online? As usual, nothing came to mind. He pounded the top of the railing with his fist, and then slowly turned and made his way back to his room.

So much was unknown in his "new" world that it frustrated him. He needed answers. He needed a direction. He sat on his bed, opened his laptop and started searching.

When it came to career options, he found more than he'd expected. And immediately felt guilty for not listening more to his therapist and getting to this point weeks ago. What was he good at? Before his accident, he was said to be good with people. He'd been charismatic, and even now he would love a career that would keep him away from the 9-to-5 desk-job routine. Sure, some office time was fine, but he'd like to be outside and moving as much as possible.

Landscaping came back to mind. Could he make a go of something like that? He'd always been good with his hands, building and growing things. But there was hardly decent money in that for a one-man operation. But at least in Texas, it wasn't a seasonal occupation, like in many other parts of the world. Winter was a cooler season here, not for planting … but it would keep him outside and physically active. It was also a job that dealt with people. He was very good with money, and of course, he had to be very good if he planned to go out on his own. He wasn't so much a salesman, but he did know that people liked to get a good deal.

Real estate crossed his mind. He could become an agent. The only thing was, the market was volatile. Lots of time was involved, encouraging each potential buyer into signing a purchase contract, and it was not a stable income.

He could drive a truck—he had certainly driven a lot of them before. But did he want to do that long-term? Or make a clean break from his past and find something new?

He closed the laptop, got up and left his room. He went down the far hallway to give himself a little more exercise. His leg felt punchy today and in need of a little extra push. Like everything, he needed balance. Something he'd do well to remember moving forward.

As he walked past the row of staff offices, his prosthetic limb gave him some trouble. He leaned against the wall to adjust it slightly.

Then heard Sandra's name.

"Has she had a follow-up meeting about Cole not taking his medications that time?" a woman asked from the room he had just passed.

He froze.

"I think so. It's not her fault. Here people don't hide what they are doing. All the medical personnel stress the importance of honesty and truth from day one with each patient. So does Dani at intake time. It's in all the brochures too."

"Well, she should have looked," the woman said, her tone exasperated. "She's the one who gives out the medicine. None of us are here all the time, so we must rely on good and accurate and complete records. As far as we know, all medications have been taken. How are we to know any different? How are we to accurately assess our patients without this data?"

"How many times do you think, since Hathaway House first opened some seven years ago, somebody has tried to trick us like Cole did?"

"No idea—but even once is too many."

"Don't be so hard on her. If she'd never run into anybody like Cole, she wouldn't be expecting that."

"Yes, but it is still her mandate, not only to give out the medicine but also to make sure they take it. Anybody can hand out tablets. It's her responsibility to administer the medicine, not just dump it out somewhere and walk out."

"Don't you think she was punished enough?"

"Was she punished?" The woman's voice lightened slightly. "If she was, well, that's good. I don't mean a major punishment. I don't think she should lose her job over it, but a reprimand is certainly in order. Not to mention a follow-up to make sure she won't do that again."

Cole's legs suddenly felt very rubbery. He had asked her in passing, way back when, if she'd gotten into trouble over him not taking his medications. Of course, when he was originally here, it had never occurred to him to consult someone. He had figured he was an adult and he had the right to take his medicine, or not, as he deemed fit.

But now, he understood that the medical world did not view it the same way. What he should have done was had a discussion with his doctor about his meds, asking which ones he could stop taking and how to wean off them. That way everybody would have been on the same page. Obviously he must have known that what he was doing was wrong because he didn't do it openly. He didn't contact the doctor. He didn't mention it to Sandra. In fact, he'd hidden it from her.

And that made him feel even worse.

The conversation behind him turned to a different topic, and he slowly moved forward. Now he was damned sorry he'd taken this hallway. All he wanted to do was go back to his room and shut the door. How would he face Sandra again, knowing she still faced reprimands from his actions? She wasn't the one who had done something stupid. That had been him. He was 100 percent responsible. No way could he let her take the fall for that.

He grabbed his phone and found his doctor under Contacts. As luck would have it, his doctor answered and said he had about fifteen minutes between patients and would come to Cole's room.

Dr. Herzog was very patient and listened to Cole explain how wrong he was to stop his meds without telling anyone and how it wasn't Sandra's fault and that he didn't want her getting into trouble. The doctor smiled at Cole. "I agree with you. However, she was reprimanded, and notice of such is in her permanent personnel file." When Cole grimaced, Dr. Herzog added, "However, in my letter I count Sandra as one of my best nurses."

When Cole launched into more arguments about how

unfair this was to punish Sandra for Cole's mistakes, Dr. Herzog raised his hand. "The people who matter know Sandra's heart. Even though she has one strike in her file, she's already redeemed herself with her updated protocols. Just like you, Cole, have one strike in your file and have already redeemed yourself with your updated actions and mind-set."

When Dr. Herzog checked his watch and said he had to leave, Cole felt drained. And frustrated.

He would try again. He picked up his phone and called Dani.

Chapter 12

SEVERAL DAYS LATER Sandra realized something really was wrong between her and Cole, and she wasn't just imagining it. She stood in his doorway and studied him. He had deliberately looked out the window as if to avoid her. She'd let him get away with it earlier but not a second time.

"Cole, may I come in?"

He turned, gave her a fake laugh. "Oh, I didn't see you standing there."

She leaned against the doorjamb, waiting for his permission to enter, and asked quietly, "What's wrong?"

He shook his head. "Nothing. Just tired. That's all."

Only he'd said that yesterday too. At first she'd believed him. But not now. Taking a chance, she strode in. "I don't believe you."

He opened his mouth to say something, but she quickly interrupted.

"Yesterday you said the same thing. Now you're ignoring me. Have I done something to upset you?"

His startled gaze focused on her. "No. Not at all."

"Then what? Why?" She motioned to the doorway. "I thought we were getting somewhere as friends." She swallowed painfully. She'd rather be upfront and honest. "I thought we were better than just friends."

His gaze softened. "It's me, not you."

She gave a sarcastic laugh and turned toward the doorway. "Right. Normally that's the woman's line." She walked out into the hall. She could feel herself shaking with hurt even while she tried to understand his attitude. Something was obviously bothering him, but what was it? And what did it have to do with her?

To bury the pain, she buried herself in her job, focusing on every detail, keeping thoughts of him, of them, at bay. There was no *them*, not really. He was just a patient, someone she'd once been friends with.

And that sucked.

COLE WATCHED SANDRA walk out, feeling like an idiot. His heart was full of regret, and he didn't know how to get back on track. He'd come here to pull himself together, but right now, he'd hit yet another major obstacle in the road. Instead of moving forward as a cohesive unit, emotionally and physically, he was breaking apart, becoming less than what he had been. He hadn't meant to hurt her feelings. He'd never do that. He really cared about her. The hurt in his heart right now made him realize he wanted more than he'd first assumed. For that reason alone, he needed to be the best he could be. She deserved nothing less.

There was a hard knock on his door. He found Brock standing in the doorway, his arms crossed over his chest, a frown on his face—not a welcoming look.

"Trouble?" Brock asked.

Maybe it was the timing, maybe it was Cole's lack of defenses. Maybe it was the new understanding about where he was right now, but he nodded. Normally he wouldn't speak about his personal problems. But over these last six months since the IED explosion, a lot had happened to change that. He could no longer be an island. He had the support of his medical team here. He would love to have Sandra's support plus he needed his friend's continued support.

"Just a really ugly realization." He leaned back on his bed and gave Brock a weak smile, who now looked the epitome of vibrant life and health. "Didn't I always compete with you? Always try to do better than you?" he asked his friend.

Brock chuckled and walked inside. He grabbed a chair, which he pivoted and sat on backward to stare at his buddy. "Not only did you always view me as competition but you always had to be of equal value." He shook his head. "No matter how I tried to convince you that you would find greatness just as you were, you didn't see that."

Cole shifted his gaze to the window. "Sometimes you have to wonder what makes a man who he is."

"Don't wonder. Accept who you are and work on changing what needs improvement. Not only did you always try to compete and to do better and to be the best," Brock said with a grin, "but you also used to hold me up as some sort of a role model. I was never that. I was never above you. I was never better than you or smarter or faster. Yet, you seemed to think that, and you always worked harder and harder to beat me."

Cole smiled. "Those were the days, weren't they?"

"They were. But you know something? I'm happy with these days too," Brock said. "I sleep in my own bed, and I have a whole new future. I have a beautiful relationship. I'm not fanatical about fitness, but I care enough to work out and to stay in shape. No, I'm not doing the same work, but I'll find something else." He shrugged. "The pressure is off right now. I hadn't realized how wearying it was being in the navy, doing what we did. We were always primed to be the best, to be in the best shape and to be ready to take on the world. Now I get to relax. I don't think I ever did that before. It never seemed like I wanted to. But I do now. Life operates at a new pace, and I like it."

"It's not the life we used to live," Cole said. "I feel different inside. When I first arrived at Hathaway, I still had that same strong drive to do bigger and better things. But there was a panic behind it. Almost a frantic need to prove I could do this." He nodded sheepishly. "And yes, I still had that sense of having to do at least as well as you did."

He motioned toward Brock, adding, "But it's also obvious this is one challenge I have to tackle differently. I don't need to be better than you," Cole said, "but I sure as hell don't want to be any less physically. I don't want poor results. I know this part is completely under my control, and yet in another way, I have no control. I can't get around the physical disabilities. Also, I was careless and hurt someone and caused trouble on my first arrival," he admitted. "I never once thought about anybody else. I never considered I would get somebody else in trouble." He shook his head. "I don't know how to fix this."

Brock raised an eyebrow. "Tell me what's going on."

Cole winced. "It's not very pretty."

"Nothing about any of what we're going through is pretty. From soiling the bed because we had no control when we woke up from surgery, to having catheters stuck up our dicks, to having nurses who wash us until we are capable of handling our own physical needs," Brock said in a harsh voice. "I've been there too, buddy. But you and I are both past that. There shouldn't be any embarrassment for either of us anymore. We know each other as well as we know anybody, so give. What the hell's going on in that head of yours?"

"It's stupid."

"It's all stupid. That also means it can and should be sorted out. Do you think I was any different when I came here, completely riddled with guilt that I wasn't blown up on the job? That I was injured in a car accident at home? Look at all the tours I did in Iraq and Afghanistan. How many opportunities I had to get some horrific physical injury. But no, I came back and got messed up driving from point A to B. I took it out on everyone," he admitted. "So don't tell me about stupid. I was stupid. Now let's hear your stupidity and see if we can get rid of it, and then hopefully you can heal that much more."

"I want to get better," Cole admitted ruefully.

Brock grinned. "Have you noticed something? It's like there are these little bars. We climb up to a certain point, and then something comes that we must deal with, and the bar falls a bit, and then we climb a little bit higher. The higher I went, the more I saw how much my personality and internal issues had to do with it. I felt like I was less than a man and not capable of being what Sidney needed," he said, shaking his head. "Wow, that was a big one."

Cole stared at him with rising hope. "I've been wondering about that myself."

"Sandra?"

Cole nodded. "We've been dancing around a lot of issues," he said, "but I hurt her, and this morning I brushed her away because I didn't know how to deal with what was in my head."

"From the beginning of your rehab, forget about everything else. Deal with one issue at a time," Brock said. He crossed his arms on the back of the chair. "We used to do this in the military. Hash out ideas, hash out our problems, hash out the little things so they didn't become bigger issues. Do it now."

Cole took a deep breath. "A few days ago I went for a short walk, feeling antsy. As I was coming back to my room, I went the long way around, past the offices. I was having some trouble with my prosthesis, so I stopped and leaned against a wall to fix it and overheard part of a conversation."

Brock nudged him along. "About you?"

"Indirectly, yes. But directly about Sandra."

Brock settled back. "Okay."

Cole continued. "About her making a mistake in her job or not having done her job properly or however it was worded. I don't remember because once I understood what it was all about, I felt really, really bad." He motioned with his hand around the room and added, "I did mention it to her at one point, weeks and weeks ago, but she brushed it off."

"She brushed what off? What did you do?"

"Remember when I first arrived, and I had that setback?"

Brock nodded. "Yes."

"Of course that setback was my fault because I was doing too much, too fast, right?"

Brock shrugged. "If you say so. I don't know the details. I know I didn't get a chance to see you. You were here and not doing so well, and then you were gone."

Cole winced. "I was so sure I knew what I needed. So sure I could handle everything that came at me. So sure that if you could do it I could do it," he muttered. "So sure that I stopped taking all the medications Sandra brought me."

"Without talking to anybody about it?" Brock leaned forward and stared at his buddy. "Without discussing this with your doctor or Sandra?"

Cole shook his head. "Exactly," he said. "Obviously it was wrong."

Brock settled back. "Wow."

"Exactly, *wow*." Filled with a sense of relief now that he'd gotten the worst of it out, he tried to explain further. "I don't understand what was going on in my head, but I thought it was a good idea. I was on a medication cocktail at the time. I hadn't had any improvement for a long time, from my perspective, and the pills didn't seem to be doing whatever it was they were supposed to. I knew I was still on some antibiotics and a few other things." He winced. "Now, of course, after the setback, and after the warnings the doctors gave me, I know I shouldn't stop taking prescription medicine suddenly."

"You had a lot of internal injuries too. When you got here, they were a little afraid it was too early for you to be in rehab as it was."

Cole nodded. "Plus, I had trouble with blood coagulation." He smiled, embarrassed. "Let's just say it was not my brightest move. The fact that I did it for three days in a row and then collapsed and had to be rushed to the hospital, well, that was the height of stupidity."

Brock nodded. "All because you figured you knew better."

"I know." Cole lifted his hands in a bewildered gesture and then let them drop in his lap. "I figured I was here now for recovery, and I didn't want anything left over from the previous hospital, including the meds, and that I could do this alone. I thought, *I can be strong. I can be fit. I can be better than everyone.*"

"Instead, you did something that worked against you and your plans."

Cole gave a bark of laughter. "Yeah, when you look at it that way, it doesn't sound so smart, does it?"

"Buddy, I hate drugs of any kind. You know that. But when I'm here, and I'm recovering from a multitude of various surgeries, and they tell me I need to take something, I take it. I mean, if I was working with bombs and you told me to put this wire on this detonator and to hold my thumb there and not to take it off, you sure as hell know I'll do that until you tell me it's safe to take my finger off."

"I know. Believe me. I know. I had lots of time in the hospital to figure that out," Cole said. "It was quite an awakening to see how much of a brain fog I had been in about what my condition was and what my future looked like." He shook his head. "I look back now, and I want to slap myself for being so stupid."

"So, what's this got to do with Sandra?"

The corners of Cole's lips turned down. "She's the one who hands out the medications every day."

Brock looked at him for a long moment and then slowly nodded. "So, she's probably been given a reprimand for not having noticed or not having stayed behind to make sure she saw you take your medications."

Cole nodded. "Something like that. I did mention it to her, and I did apologize way back when, and she seemed to brush it off. However, in the hallway, I heard them talking about how she's doing her job since that event."

"And about you?"

"About me and other patients. I got the impression it

was whether she had changed up her procedure enough since the warning to get her off the hook."

Brock winced. "Sandra's been here a long time."

"All I had to do was talk to the doctor to find out how many of them were necessary, and why I was taking them, and which ones I needed to take, and which I could try to get off," Cole said. "But to go off drugs like that—it's not safe to go cold turkey."

Brock sighed.

"Yeah stupid I know, I've figured that out now."

"You always were a bit of a hard-headed 'jump first and think later' guy. But right now, I presume you're feeling crappy about what you did, and added to that, you might have gotten Sandra into trouble. Even if it's a done deal for you, it might not be over for her."

Cole slowly nodded. "It's not. Even though I spoke to Dr. Herzog to straighten it all out, I was too late. When I came back here the second time, all I wanted to do was to forget about that horrible start. Everybody joked about my restart, and yet it doesn't appear that Sandra got her reboot. I never meant to get her in trouble, Brock. You've gotta believe me. I would never do that. She's great at her job. She loves being here. She served all these people so well, and yet here I come along, and in three days, I completely mess up her life."

"But it doesn't seem like she's holding it against you. She's been more than friends with you for the last month. She's been your confidant and something a whole lot closer from the looks of it, and at the same time this has been going on in the background in her world."

"And she didn't share it with me."

"That's another part that's gotten to you, isn't it? She

knows more about you than you do about her, including that she was in trouble over this."

Cole lay against the headboard and nodded. "Exactly."

Brock crossed his arms over his chest. "On that aspect, you're not thinking clearly. She's in a position where she's the guardian of your health. She's the watchdog. She's got to make sure what she sees and registers as your results on a day-to-day basis is factual and truthful, so she does the absolute best she can to minimize any negative impacts on your health. For that reason alone, she wouldn't tell you, knowing guilt will have a detrimental effect on you and your healing."

Cole stared at him. "You see? I know that ... but my heart doesn't like it."

"Got it. It doesn't change the fact, however, that if I were in her position, I wouldn't have said anything to you either, bro," Brock said.

Cole stared at his buddy for a long moment, then slowly nodded. "I guess I see your point. If our situations were reversed, and I thought she would be injured by the information and it would slow her healing, I wouldn't tell her either."

"Do you understand how much of a chance she's taking, being friends with you and dealing with all of this? She hasn't had an easy time of it, and now you've made it harder on her. Maybe that's something you should take a closer look at. Because she's here and available doesn't mean you can hurt her willingly either."

"Not willingly," Cole protested.

"Unknowingly or not, your actions have a domino effect on others. Not just her either."

"Do you think she did wrong?" Cole hated that he had

to ask. He really hated that. He wanted to defend her to the ends of the earth, but he didn't know what he was supposed to do.

"No, I don't. She gave you the medicine, and you're an adult. You were cognizant and in your right mind. You were under no force, no duress. She shouldn't be in trouble." Brock shook his head. "However, you hid what you were doing, so she couldn't document anything. You didn't talk to her, so she couldn't report it either. The worst of it is that she wasn't as observant as she should've been."

Cole stared at the doorway. "She put it on the table and left."

"That's all she should have to do. Because, if you don't want to take it, that's up to you. Step up and take the responsibility for your healing, or your non-healing, and be responsible for your actions," Brock said quietly. "She's paying for the repercussions of your actions. She also must stand up and take the repercussions for her own actions. If it was not in her mandate to stay and watch as every patient swallows their pills, then she won't be in trouble."

"And yet, she does that now."

Brock looked at him and nodded. "Of course she does. As you came close to dying, she's not sure how your mental stability was back then, and as for the medications, well, you never talked about it with her. So, it's her responsibility now to make sure it doesn't happen again. She has changed her system, and because of that, she has taken on more responsibility to make sure patients are taking their medications."

Inside, Cole could feel his whole sense of complacency at being at Hathaway sinking. He leaned back and stared out the window. "Maybe it would have been better if I hadn't come at all."

"I have been there too," said Brock. "When we are injured and hurting, and we have that support network around us, it's easy to believe the world revolves around us," he said. "We are unaware of what our actions lead to and what it is that we set in motion, as well as how we feel about it." He shook his head. "That will work to a point. Then we switch from 'me' to 'we,' as the team helps us move through this process. But the medical staff are real people, just like us. They have weaknesses and strengths, just as we do."

"And is there another stage? Where it's back to 'me' again without the 'we'?"

At that, Brock bounced to his feet. "Absolutely. That's where I'm at. So just keep working through the process, and remember these people are here to help you, one way or another."

"What about my heart? What about when our heart is feeling a whole lot more than it should?"

"I don't know that there is such a thing as too much heart. Part of that 'me to we and back' transition is all about accepting help. About accepting friendships and taking the ones that matter the most and moving forward. It's not wrong to care. It's never wrong to care." He walked to the doorway. "I'm going to sit outside. Want to come with me?"

Cole stared at Brock for a long moment. "You know? I think I'll go to the pool. I love being in it, and I have stuff inside to be worked out."

Brock smiled. "Talk to you later then, my friend."

Chapter 13

SANDRA SAT AT her desk to attack some paperwork finally. Kenneth had left—an added bonus for her. Plus she'd spent so much time with Cole lately she had more recordkeeping backed up than she liked. She hadn't shirked her job, but she could have done more, and if she hadn't had other interests, she'd have done this already. Now was a good time to get caught up.

At least it gave her something to focus on, other than the hurt inside.

Shane sat on the chair beside her. "Tell me what's going on."

She looked up in surprise and caught sight of the clock behind his head. She'd been here for two hours already. She turned her attention back to Shane. "Nothing's going on. Why would you think that?" She tried hard to keep her voice calm and stable, but there was an ever-so-slight tremor. When understanding came into his eyes, she groaned and sat back, flinging down her pen. "Okay, so something is wrong but nothing major, and I'll get over it."

"Something to do with your meeting later this afternoon or did something happen with Cole?"

She frowned. "I've been trying to forget about this afternoon's meeting." And she had for the most part. It was a follow-up to the initial problem Sandra had had with Cole.

"Well, that answers that. It's Cole."

She shook her head. "Not so much about Cole as understanding that the men here are complicated."

Shane grinned. "I'm not all that simple myself."

She rolled her eyes. "You know what I mean."

He nodded. "Yes, I do. The patients all come here with an awful lot of issues. That also makes the price that much sweeter when you get there, reaching the goal."

She laughed wryly. "Well, that would be nice today as he said a few hurtful things this morning. I let him get to me."

"So maybe look at why he's pushing you away. What it is he thinks he's done, or in what way does he think he's failed? It's either that or he has decided you're better off without him."

She sat back in surprise. "Surely not all relationships can be reduced to those options."

He shook his head. "Of course not. That doesn't stop it from being true most of the time. In many cases, it is exactly something like that. Especially here. These men were prime specimens—big egos, big bodies, fit, capable and powerful—until an injury sidelined them. Some come with an attitude they can take on anything, and they do. It's wonderful to see them storm right through their healing and recovery process." He smiled. "Others charge ahead and fall back because they took too many big steps at once."

"Cole." Hence her upcoming meeting this afternoon. She shook her head. "But he won't do that again. He's not the same guy anymore."

"Good, glad to hear that. Do you think Cole got wind of your reprimand about his actions?"

"No. That's strictly a doctor-nurse thing. It's part of my job, and I screwed up."

"What if somebody mentioned it to him? What if somebody told him, either laughingly or jokingly, that because of him, you got into trouble?" He leaned forward. "Do you think that would make him feel good or bad?"

"With Cole, that would make him feel terrible. He's already thinking he's not enough. That if he hadn't driven over an IED, he wouldn't be here."

"That's a running theme with a lot of the men here. They were either taken out during a mission and feel guilty or injured during some stupid thing stateside and feel equally guilty because it wasn't on a mission."

"Of course that's Brock." She sighed. "I'm not even upset at Cole about his initial screw-up. It's just that when you open yourself up to a person, it hurts to get slapped back down again."

"And yet, you're coming from reasonably healthy relationships in your past. For you, opening up isn't such a big deal. That's your nature. Neither is that big slap in the long run as you evolve. Ignore your hurt for a moment. Look at the bigger picture and figure out why he's doing this. Then get him to explain it to you. Because that shows you trust him. He must slowly rebuild who he is, what he is and what he wants. He'll make mistakes along the way. As you build a relationship with him, you can make mistakes along the way too."

She gave Shane a warm smile. "How did you become so smart?"

COLE FELT A lot better after talking with Brock. He also knew he owed Sandra an apology. She had appeared so upbeat about the whole thing, but then again, he'd been so mired in his own thoughts and feelings he hadn't taken any time to see where she was coming from. He lay on his bed and stared out the window. One of the good things about being here was his sleep had improved. He realized just how much so when he looked back on the long journey he'd taken since the accident. In the beginning, he had regularly woken up in a cold sweat after recurring nightmares, but now things had calmed down.

He had turned that around and had made many positive steps forward. He was slowly moving away from the nightmares. People had warned him about PTSD and said the effects could hit him anytime down the road. It was awfully hard on relationships too. But so far, that hadn't been a big issue for him. Just that horrible feeling of having to catch up to others. Otherwise the world would leave him behind.

He shook his head. Maybe that was rooted in his childhood. He was the youngest of three brothers. Coming fifteen years after his next oldest brother, Cole had always felt left behind, which was true in a sense, and how they were years ahead of him, which was also true. He had little to no relationship with them, then or now. They already had girlfriends who later morphed into wives. But he'd spent so much of his childhood trying to catch up to them.

He felt that way when he had become a Navy SEAL too.

How odd. He hadn't made that connection before.

He'd made it through basic training, and they were some of the best days of his life. Afterward with Brock and Denton at his side, things had gotten even better—having buddies who accepted him was great. However, he always worried he was inferior and thought he couldn't compare to them. Then Brock had his accident. Brock appeared to fall so far down that, for once, Cole didn't fall short when compared to Brock. Cole didn't have to "catch up" to close the gap between how he saw the two of them.

He felt small admitting that about Brock. At least it wasn't a conscious thought. It was more a case of being able to relax because he didn't have to work so hard to catch up to Brock anymore. The same was true when Denton got injured.

Until Cole had his own accident. That led him to the same lack of self-confidence and acceptance he had known over his whole life.

So was he doomed to relive his childhood fears comparing himself to his brothers in all his later relationships in life?

Yet, his brothers were never really *in* his life, already moving on to lives of their own by the time Cole was old enough to have memories of them. His parents had "moved on" too, both dying months apart, shortly after he turned twenty.

He needed to book time with his therapist to work out some of this. Since he'd been here, and since he'd seen the shape Brock was now in, Cole was so far behind again, which was where his depression and angst came from. He didn't know if Sandra would understand this, and he didn't want to cry on her shoulder, to explain all this heavy stuff because he really liked her. He didn't want her to see him like this, weak. He wanted her to see him as a strong physical male with a can-do attitude. All this heavy emotional crap would be a burden on anybody.

The last thing he wanted was to dump it on her.

He picked up his phone and sent a text to his therapist. He didn't have an appointment scheduled for the next couple days, but it suddenly seemed important that he deal with this sooner rather than later. He grabbed the notebook Dani had given him and jotted down ideas. He could see how so much of this was rooted in his childhood, but that didn't mean he wanted to continue repeating this. What he needed was to stop feeling so inferior. To stop feeling he wasn't good enough. To stop feeling he had to constantly improve and be better to be accepted.

He had thought for sure that making it through BUD/s training would help him gain that self-confidence. Making the final cut for BUD/s proved that. Plus the BUD/s training had been plenty hard. BUD/s took only the best of the best, and he had been one of those. For a long time, it seemed like he'd been okay with that. Having Denton and Brock around had been a huge help too. Together, they'd formed a friendship that would last for life.

Yet, he didn't remember his current insecurities ever being an issue before between the three of them because they'd all helped each other. It wasn't him against the world anymore, nor was it about his older brothers being so far ahead of him, not waiting for their kid brother to catch up. With Brock and Denton, it was the three of them together against the world, and Cole had been happy there.

He had been comfortable, content. No—it had been—and he wrote down the word as it came to him—*secure*. He'd lost that feeling after the accident. He had lost his place in the world. It was like he'd lost his place in his SEAL family too. The family dynamics had changed when Brock had been injured and while he was gone, but Cole still had Denton. Although they had kept in touch with Brock, he wasn't there physically, and he wasn't there mentally. Yet, that had been okay. Cole's SEAL family unit had shifted and changed, but it was still complete.

And then Cole had been injured and Denton too, and Cole had lost that sense of family security. When he'd arrived here, he had immediately jumped forward, trying to "catch up" again—to his SEAL family this time. Trying to regain his place beside Brock. Chasing his brothers again. Only Cole had lagged so damn far behind, he panicked that he wouldn't make it. He had to give it his all. But of course, instead of talking to anybody about it, he was full of bravado and had dumped his medicine with the idea that he didn't need it.

He thought he could do this without any outsiders' help. Because he knew he could, because he was so macho and so male. Sure, in the past, in the military, that was the way things were done. SEAL teams against whoever else. But this was a whole new world, and he didn't know how to find his place in it. As he jotted down these notes, that was another key point. He had been left standing on quicksand. He had lost his footing, his foundation, and while that was one of his key points, he'd also lost so much more. Not only was he on shaky ground physically, but he was on shaky ground emotionally and mentally. He thought about it and added *spiritually* to that sentence too. He sat back, realizing tremors ran up and down his system.

Talk about home truths.

Talk about ugly home truths …

He shook his head. He hadn't expected some of this to come up. As he stared out the window, he wondered what it would take for that little boy inside to be comfortable with the man who he was now and with his position in the world. When would the little boy from his childhood stop trying so hard for all the wrong reasons?

Try? Yes.

Work hard? Yes.

But do it because it was important to him in his own world, not because he was "catching up" to be like the others.

There was a knock on his door. Inside he hoped whoever it was would walk away. He wanted to be alone right now. So much was going on inside him, like his support walls were crumbling. He was vulnerable. He opened his mouth to tell them to go away, but his therapist stepped inside and smiled at him.

Her gaze sharpened. She turned, closed the door and grabbed the spare chair. She reached out for his hand, and he grabbed on. She sat beside him. "I see you've had a break-through."

He stared at her, his fingers clenching hers. He was in his early thirties, and this woman had to be in her mid-fifties. But her grip was solid. It was like a lifeline at this moment in time when he felt like he was drowning.

"A breakthrough?" he said in a broken voice. "How is this possibly a breakthrough?"

She smiled and gently squeezed his fingers with her own. "Tell me ..."

And the crumbling walls burst, and the words poured out.

Chapter 14

S ANDRA GLANCED AT her watch. It was time. She'd avoided thinking about it for most of the day, her mind consumed with what was going on with Cole. She didn't know what the hell she would do about him. But she couldn't worry about that now. She got up, grabbed a notebook and poured herself a cup of coffee from the pot in the nurses' station before walking to her meeting. The doctor was already there ahead of her, as was Dani. Sandra smiled at them both and sat.

After the initial pleasantries, the conversation kicked to the subject of Cole.

"Personally I'm delighted with his progress," Dr. Herzog said. "After that rough start, he seems to be settling in quite nicely and is showing a lot of improvements on many levels."

He turned to look at Dani and Sandra.

Dani nodded. "I agree. He's approached me a couple times on things that were bothering him. I take his ability to ask for help and question some of those issues as a good step forward. He has taken responsibility for his own healing. He is looking at his recovery now with a more independent spirit. He's gone from 'me' to dependency on the team, but I do see glimmers that he is looking outward at the bigger world and his role in it."

"You always see the best things," Sandra said. "He is

looking at the world like you described."

Dani smiled. "Well, it's true. There are so many stages to the recovery process. Everybody doesn't go through all of them, but they all get to the healing part, eventually—we hope."

The doctor faced Sandra. "How do you feel about his medications?"

She nodded. "I'm making sure he's taking all of them, Doctor. I've dealt with the fact that I was partially responsible for his decline."

"It's good that you feel you have dealt with your part but not that you feel even partially responsible. He's a grown man who made his own decisions, and now he has recovered and moved on," he said. "Dani, I think we're done here, unless you have any concerns?"

Dani shook her head. "No, not at all. The issue was brought up. It was addressed. We moved on." Dani turned toward Sandra. "Cole's concerned about any ramifications his actions may have had on you."

Sandra's eyebrows shot upward. "Really? Must have been a few days ago then," she said drily. "I'm not even sure he is talking to me today."

"If he doesn't," Dani said, "maybe he'll tell Brock whatever is bothering him."

"That brings up an interesting point," the doctor said. "How do you feel about them being friends here? Has it been a benefit or a detriment? Does Brock's presence help Cole, or does it make it worse for him?"

"I think it makes things easier for him," Sandra said. "But at the same time, I think he held Brock up as a bit of an idol, with his progress as the goalposts. Brock has achieved exactly what Cole desperately wants to do," she said. "I think

Brock's improvement pushed Cole's competitiveness so far and so fast that that is why he made that error in judgment with his meds and all. I think he's moved past that." She glanced around. "Maybe we should bring the rest of the team in for that discussion."

"I've heard their comments at the weekly team meetings, and you two are currently seeing progress as do I." The doctor made several notations in the file and then handed it to Dani. "If that's it, I'm heading out." He gathered his things, said his farewells and walked out.

Sandra felt stunned. She leaned toward Dani. "That's it?"

Dani looked at her, a smile playing at the corner of her lips. "What were you expecting? Another reprimand?"

She frowned at her. "Frankly, yes."

"Have you had any further issues that are a direct result of the initial incident?" Dani asked.

"No, of course not," Sandra replied.

"Therefore, no new reprimand. We all trust you to do your job. Continue to follow your changed methodology. There is no need for anything else."

Sandra frowned at her good friend. "You do realize I've been a bit worried about this since Cole's original setback?"

"You do realize you should calm down about it and not worry?" was Dani's reply. "At least not to that extent. But it is to your credit that you are as concerned about it as you are. It's nice to know that you care enough to make sure you're doing what you can for your patients."

"I love it here," Sandra said. "At the beginning, I was terrified I would get fired, but apparently that's not an issue."

"Once again, only one person has to take responsibility

for this, and that would be Cole. We must look at his actions. And nobody ever once suggested you should be fired."

Sandra sat back in her chair, a sense of relief coursing through her. "I didn't expect that, but I did expect to be warned about that eventuality."

"Would you feel better if we did warn you that you could lose your job?"

Sandra thought about it. "That would be foolish. Like I hadn't thought of the repercussions myself. Like I was afraid to trust my own judgment as to how to correct the issue." She shook her head. "No, I definitely don't want that. I've had no problems here for five years, then one patient comes along, and everything goes to hell." She laughed. "Of course it would be Cole."

"One more thing I want to be clear on. Have you had any disparaging remarks from any of your coworkers as a result of this situation?" Dani asked.

At that, Sandra shook her head.

"Good. If you do, please let me know." Dani rose and said, "By the way, you may want to see this." She held out the file the doctor had given her, opened to the topmost page. Sandra could see right off that it was her personnel file because her name was on the side. At the bottom of the page, the doctor had written, "Excellent nurse. You would be wise to keep her here."

Dani laughed, closed the file and made her way across the room. She turned in the doorway. "If you're still out of sorts, maybe go see Stan. I know one of his assistants had to leave early today. I imagine he's a little on the short-staffed side."

Sandra checked her watch. Considering she had just gotten off easily—to her way of thinking—she could certainly help out Stan. He had been a huge support for her in this situation. She made her way downstairs to see Rebecca, Stan's assistant out in front, dealing with several frustrated-looking customers. She walked around to the back of the counter and leaned over.

"Is there anything I can do?" she whispered.

The assistant nodded with relief. "I'm all right out here, but Stan needs help in Exam Room 2."

Sandra smiled and pushed open the door to the room in question. Stan was inside with an owner and a very large dog, who was whining and squirming on the table.

"Oh, dear," she said as she approached Stan. "May I help?"

He looked at her with gratitude. "We've given Rocky his shots, but I could use your help in the back. We're behind on feedings and cleaning the cages. I don't have my assistant today, who normally does those two jobs. If you only clean out the cages, that'd be huge."

She smiled. "I'm used to cleaning up messes. No problem."

Sandra walked into the back to see that at least ten of the cages were full. She'd been here many times over the years and knew exactly what had to be done. She started with a female cat that had been spayed. She was still groggy, but she was scheduled to be picked up before the end of the day. Sandra gave her a quick cleanup, checked on her to make sure she was okay and left her to recover. Sandra could clean that cage once she was gone.

After that, it was a case of systematically going through, reading the charts and instructions, changing out newspapers, towels and bedding and checking on each of the patients to make sure they were recovering well. She also gave each one a little bit of love and attention so they would be reassured everything was okay. The animals were scared—some of them were in pain, and most of them were groggy from drugs. Two of them were on IVs.

Once she'd checked all bandages, she then changed each animal's water dish. She filled up food dishes, changed some cages, and before she knew it, she was done. The room itself also needed to be cleaned as some bloody towels were left on the table, and all kinds of paper towels were crumpled into a heap on one side of the floor. She took a moment to clean up the back room. When she was done, she walked out to the much quieter reception area. "Okay, cages done, back cleaned, rooms tidied up. What else can I do?"

Rebecca looked at her. "You're an angel. Do you have time to walk these two dogs?" She pointed to the two patient charts in her hands. "They both need to go outside."

"How long are they here for?"

"They both belong to the same owner, but he's been called away on a family emergency, so the dogs are staying overnight."

Sandra headed toward the dog pen on the other side of the room. She clipped leashes on both of the spaniels, and the two bounced around her legs in delight. Leading them through the back, she headed down the tracks toward the pastures. If she was taking them for a walk, she might as well enjoy it and be outside in the sunshine, walking in the areas where she could partake of the beautiful weather too. She didn't want to rush the dogs because they would be closed up again for the rest of the evening. Of course, somebody would take them out again in the morning, but without their owners and being in a strange place, it wasn't much fun for them either.

She took her time and let them sniff all around. When they had both done their business, she cleaned up with the doggie bags she had shoved into her pocket and slowly led the animals back to the clinic. When she got them in their cages, she stayed with them for a few minutes as they settled in. Then she washed her hands and returned to reception.

Stan came to say goodbye to a patient and to drop off two files at the front counter. He turned for the next patient and stopped. "Nobody else is on the list?"

The receptionist smiled. "You're done for the day, Stan."

He chuckled wryly and clapped his hands together. "Thank God for that." He turned to Sandra. "And I see you've been a busy bee. You managed to sweep up and wash down the back room as well as take care of our furry friends."

She laughed. "I needed to keep busy," she confessed.

A knowing look came into his eyes. "Problems with Cole?"

She grinned, feeling slightly embarrassed. "You say that like it's a common occurrence."

"Not so much a common occurrence with you," he said. "But a common occurrence with the women at Hathaway in general at the moment. I've had both Dani and Sidney down here with the same issues."

She winced. "Yes, your clinic has become quite the remedy for us when our spirits are low."

He shrugged. "I have nothing against that. I wish more of the patients would come here. They'd probably heal a lot faster."

"We do try."

"Why don't you take out that big tomcat in the back?

We did some work on his paws. He had an ingrown nail that we cut out. But that's fixed, and he's very relaxed. He would also appreciate the chance to get out, I'm sure."

"Is he good with people? If so, then maybe I'll take him upstairs to visit."

"He's very good with people. By the way, his name is Juicy."

"Why would anybody name him that?"

"Because he drools." Stan gave her a droll look. "He has a harness apparently, and he is quite accustomed to it, so he might want to walk, but he won't want to walk too far. Besides he prefers being carried." He chuckled. "That could have something to do with why he's on the overweight side."

Juicy was overweight, but he was also adorable. He was a cross between a Persian and some other breed, so his face was flatter than a normal feline's profile.

As soon as she picked him up in her arms, she wanted to show him to everybody upstairs. She hit the button for the elevator, and when it opened on the top floor, she stepped out. The cat looked around with interest. Sandra walked to the far side where she knew several men who had been here for weeks. As she approached, they looked up, and a big smile broke across one man's face.

"Isn't he a fine-looking boy?"

She chuckled. "I thought I remembered you were a cat guy, Connor."

He gave her a big grin. "I so am." He reached up, and she very gently put Juicy in his lap. Connor had lost most of one arm above the elbow. But that didn't stop him from cuddling the cat and scratching Juicy's ears.

"My, look at that. This guy has a bum arm like I do." Connor chuckled.

Connor was very careful to avoid the bandage on the cat, in case Juicy was upset about it, but the cat didn't seem to care. He was placid, and as long as somebody held him, he seemed to be happy.

Sandra watched Connor interact with the other men at the table. It was amazing what good news, combined with a little animal therapy, could do for a person.

Then there was Cole. His words this morning, well, those had bothered her a lot.

But what could she do about it?

IT SEEMED LIKE hours before Cole finally ran out of words. He lay on his bed, almost dripping with exhaustion. But he hoped that feeling was internal and that his therapist didn't realize how messed up he was. Going back into his childhood, then examining the various points in this pivotal year, moving forward at her nudging—it had been an exhausting and emotional journey. He lay here, staring at his hands, so mentally tired and emotionally exhausted he wasn't sure he could add anything more.

She straightened and smiled at him. "That's quite a breakthrough, Cole."

He raised his tired gaze to her. "Good. Hopefully I don't ever have to go through that again." He managed a weak smile. "Is a breakthrough supposed to take all the stuffing out of you and make you feel like you're limp, lying on the bed without a bone or muscle left to do anything?"

She chuckled quietly. "Sometimes, yes. Sometimes it's worse. But in any case, it's all good."

He shook his head. "Yet, I don't want anything to do

with anybody anymore. I don't want to talk to people. I want to hole up and hide away. I wish I lived in a cave somewhere, a long way away."

"That's normal. When you have a breakthrough like this, you come face-to-face with parts of yourself you haven't met in a long time. It's like finding out you don't want to be alone anymore, but at the same time, not liking the people you're with."

"I still need to talk to Sandra to clear the air," he said. "But right now, I don't want anything to do with her." He shook his head. "I know that sounds horrible but ..."

"It's not so much about avoiding people as it is about you needing time to be with yourself. So you don't have to justify how you feel to me." She stood. "How about I let you rest right now? Do you need anything?" She grabbed the blanket from the foot of the bed and opened it up over him. "The best thing you can do is rest."

He nodded. "Can you clear my afternoon? I don't know if it's possible, but I'd appreciate it."

He snuggled deeper into the blanket, wishing she would go away now too. A lot of stuff swirled around in his head. Thoughts and emotions, actions, reactions, all that he had pulled out from dark, disturbed places he had to look at but didn't want to. They fascinated him but repelled him at the same time. He knew most of it was childhood stuff, painful memories from a long time ago. Instances that had made perfect sense at the time but now were the exact opposite. He truly wanted the world to go away.

As she walked to the door, he called out, "If you see anyone coming, tell them I don't want to see anyone."

He wasn't sure if the door was open already, but he heard voices outside.

She called back, "That's all right. I'll tell everybody you're not available today."

He curled up into a ball under his blanket. "Thank you."

He felt he should do something about Sandra, but he wasn't up to it. He also wasn't sure what to say now. Because of the thoughts in his heart, everything was in complete confusion. More than that, he felt so empty. Drained. There should be a sense of relief, a sense of renewal. But he didn't feel that now. He was still an empty vacuum on the inside. He wanted the world to go away. Or maybe he wanted the world to disappear with him in it. He could hear a conversation going on outside. He didn't know what the conversation was, and he didn't care. He wanted the door closed and everyone locked out.

"Please, close the door. Nobody's to come in," he called out. When he heard the *snick* as the door latched, he relaxed further. Perfect. All he wanted to do now was sleep, collapse, pass out, ignore everything and everybody. Maybe when he woke up, this would all be over, and he'd feel like a better person. Right now, he just felt like shit.

Chapter 15

SANDRA LEANED AGAINST the wall in the hallway outside Cole's room. She watched the therapist walk away. She had been told quite clearly nobody was welcome inside and Cole had mentioned her specifically.

The blow was visceral.

The therapist didn't have to say that because Sandra had already heard enough as she'd stood here at the doorway getting ready to knock. Hathaway House was well-built, but nothing could keep those harsh words from being heard where she stood. Cole didn't want to talk to her. He didn't want to see her or have anything to do with her right now.

That was hard enough.

She'd just come to terms with her own messed-up emotions and didn't need to hear that. Not only was it stunning in its timing but the effect on her psychological state was devastating. She forced herself to return to her office. To do something that could keep her mind off this morass of thoughts that threatened to break her into tears. He probably had a good reason for what he'd said. But ... well, it was too much now.

She had the last of her files and stacks of paperwork to be done. She had medicine to give out, cabinets to be sorted and tidied and new stock to be ordered. She'd do it as she always had. It was her job. She'd be the same person she always was, happy and friendly to all the patients, but at the same time there was this gap—a disconnect between her heart and her soul. A place where Cole had existed. A place that was rapidly emptying. She didn't know what had happened or why Cole had been in his room for so long, but his therapist hadn't been upset upon leaving Cole, which usually meant Kimmy had seen progress on the patient's part.

That was good. But if Sandra was part of the problem, if she was part of the old stuff he was getting rid of, well—she knew how that worked.

Unfortunately.

Drawn and tired out, she worked like an automaton, quickly pushing through the work she had to do. By the time she finished up for the day, she wasn't sure she wanted food. She knew when she got to her room and lay down, it would be worse. So she delayed going to her apartment and headed to the dining room, but it was too early for dinner yet. Maybe she could pick up something in case she got hungry later.

She had to wear off this numbness, the sense of deadness inside. Cole had taught her some things about swimming, but the pool would feel lonely without him there by her side. Still, it was a good way to take what he'd had to offer and move on. That was what he'd done—what he was doing. She'd be a fool not to do the same. It would also help her work up an appetite for dinner. She went to her room, changed and grabbed her cover-up, then went to the pool. It was busy, but the slow lane was empty.

That's just perfect, she thought. She dropped her towel and her cover-up, went to the deep end and dove in, remembering all the lessons she'd been working on this week. Slowly she made her way to the other end. She could see that she had progressed somewhat.

If she could do even ten laps, that was something. She forced herself to empty her mind and to focus on her strokes, to focus on hitting the far wall, turning and flipping back, returning to the other side. She kept on moving, left arm, right arm, left arm twisting, take a breath, face down, next stroke and repeat. She didn't remember when she'd gone from swimming with her head above water to swimming with her face underwater. She'd had a breakthrough of her own.

She didn't even get a chance to show Cole. That was how life was. You learned something, you moved on. You wanted to show people so they could share in your joy, but at the same time, even if they weren't there, you still had to push forward. The joy had to be hers. She had to be proud of herself and not simply proud for someone else or because someone else seemed proud of her.

Trying harder to shake off her mood, she poured more energy into her strokes. She used a full-leg kick, like an otter. Getting to the far end of the pool was a bigger chore than she had imagined, so she shifted her strokes so she was above water and slowly worked on her less-strenuous breaststroke. When she hit the shallow end, she walked to the ladder, and then made her way to the nearby bench. There she collapsed with her towel wrapped around her.

A few people were still around. She smiled at several as they walked past. She grabbed a second towel and rubbed her face down, but she could feel tears burning in the back of her eyes. She hated crying. It made her face all puffy and red. It made her throat dry out. But worst, it made the rest of her feel like she had been pushed through an old ringer-style washing machine. It left her feeling rubbery on the inside. She stood, grabbed her cover-up and headed back to her room. There, she showered and got dressed.

A lot of daylight hours still remained, and she didn't know what she wanted to do. Food first and then she needed an avenue to heal the hole in her soul. There was so much pain involved in letting go. She walked to the dining hall and found the room a bit more full than the last time she'd been here. A hot dinner was already laid out. She would go to bed early tonight, so an early dinner would be fine. She still had no idea how she would fill her evening hours though, not expecting to sleep at all.

Normally that wasn't a problem here. She could walk, she could sit around and watch TV or read a book or visit with some of the patients or other live-in staff. But right now she didn't want to be around anyone. She grabbed a plate and picked out a few items. She was very hungry, yet nothing appealed to her. By the time she reached the end of the buffet line, she figured she had enough nutrients to get her through the rest of the day. She walked to the other side of the dining hall and sat with her back to the room. She stared apathetically at her plate. Suddenly a man stood beside her.

She forced a smile at him. "Hi, Brock. What's up?"

He motioned at the empty chair at her table. "May I sit?"

"Sure. What are you up to?"

"Waiting for Sidney to finish work so we can have dinner together."

Sandra dropped her gaze to the table. That word *together*. It was wonderful when you were a couple with someone. But it seriously sucked when you were alone.

She pasted another bright smile on her face. "I'm happy for you two. You look like you would do well together."

He chuckled. "I hope so, but I'm not easy. At least she's not scared off by me."

"Why would she be scared off?" Sandra asked, curious.

"Because I still have bad days," he explained. "Some days I'm irrational, then I get completely overwhelmed with a lack of self-confidence, a sense of defeat and a sense of hopelessness. If it wasn't for her standing by me through the rough times, I'm sure I wouldn't have made it this far. And I certainly would have scared off any number of other potential girlfriends."

Sandra wondered if some of this was a warning for her. "Sidney is a special person. She doesn't scare easily."

"Isn't that the truth? She's some woman."

He seemed to mean it. That he was so full of admiration and joy, and just to know he was together with Sidney, brought a true smile to her face. "I'm really happy for you," she said warmly.

He looked at her, his gaze piercing. "And I'm really happy for you too."

She sat back, mostly wanting to put some distance between the two of them. "Why?"

"Because you and Cole have the basis for exactly what Sidney and I have. The trouble is, you two are back where Sidney and I were when we started. Lots of doubts and insecurities, rough days on either side, rubbing up against each other, and then pushing away. Like trying to keep magnets apart."

She winced. "Yeah, that's a little too close to the truth."

He nodded. "But that doesn't mean it has to stay that way. Cole's going through some rough times right now."

She snorted. "You think?" She shook her head. "Of course he is. It's part of his healing process."

"Just because you know that doesn't make it easy when he doesn't include you in it."

She shot him a look of surprise. "That's very perceptive of you." She shifted her gaze to the horses in the fields. "Maybe I should go for a horseback ride again tonight."

He turned and glanced at the horses as well. "That would be a lovely idea. I guess I wanted to give you a vote of confidence," he said with a brief self-conscious smile. "I don't want you to give up on Cole. Because Cole might give up on himself then. That's the worst thing any of us can do—giving up on ourselves and that someone special in our lives."

He got up and left, leaving her to her thoughts. And what a mess they were.

She watched him walk away. Did he know about Cole's breakthrough? She glanced around the room surreptitiously. Did anyone else know? The only way anybody could know is if Cole or the therapist had spoken to someone, and they'd either overheard or been that person spoken to. She sure as hell hadn't said anything. Did Cole and Brock talk to that extent?

Maybe he knew what was going on with Cole's current condition. She wanted to call Brock back and ask him if he knew what Cole's breakthrough was all about. But that would be prying. She had had his door slammed in her face over that, quite firmly. There could be no asking questions and getting personal information unless it was from Cole now. That was tough too. Brock was part of his confidence group. She thought she had been. Obviously not. Rejection was a bitch.

She settled back and stared out at the grass and the sunset. As she sat here, she realized how much of an assumption she'd made over these last weeks as she and Cole got closer and closer. She had thought they were more than friends. Heading to something much more than that. Apparently, she'd overstepped her bounds and had been drifting down a fantasy road. But then she recalled conversations and touches, the joy of being with him, the glances, the smiles. It hadn't been all on her own that she had made those assumptions. He'd been as much a part of it as she had been.

As she sat, more than sadness and despair filled her. There was a kernel of anger. She might've been responsible for where she was now, but so the hell was he. That wasn't fair. She was exhausted after her swim, but now an anger that just wouldn't go away rippled inside her, and she'd no idea what to do with it. Where could she go to avoid her anger? How would she handle this mess?

She'd never availed herself of any of the professional services offered here. Right about now, she could sure use someone. It would have to be somebody she didn't know, somebody who didn't know her situation because she'd have to work with them afterward, and that would be very difficult. She was essentially a very private person. She never aired her dirty laundry in public. But right now, she hurt. Everything hurt. She wasn't sure how she would get through tonight. The evening stretched out ahead of her endlessly, and she couldn't even begin to imagine getting through the initial hours.

COLE WOKE TO darkness in his room. He slowly rolled over

to his back. He hadn't done anything overly physical, other than his normal therapy work. But he hurt. Everywhere. Joints he hadn't noticed in the last few months were now aching. His muscles hurt—even his gut throbbed.

"What the hell was that all about?" he mumbled.

How was it that letting go of emotions and old traumas could hurt on so many deep physical levels? Yet, he finally had a sense of freedom. A sense of openness. As if he'd dropped several huge weights off his shoulders.

Which he guessed he had. He slowly sat up and lowered his legs to the floor. Grabbing his crutches, he made his way to the bathroom. As he stared at his face, he saw he even looked different. He wasn't sure if that was an improvement yet. He still had that worn-out, been-through-the-fires-of-hell look. But not in a physical way—in an emotional way.

He checked his watch and saw it was just past midnight. He shook his head in astonishment. Talk about one helluva sleeping pill. He'd been knocked out and had stayed out. He'd missed dinner, sleeping all afternoon and into the evening, and now the whole place was asleep. Where the hell was he to go? He wasn't even sure if he was ready to get up yet. His body had forced him out of bed but couldn't he just go back to sleep?

He slowly made his way to the bed and realized he was still fully dressed. He hadn't been under the covers—he'd been lying under a single blanket. Then he remembered his therapist had thrown it over him.

He wasn't sure if he'd sleep anymore, but he had to try. He undressed to his boxers and this time crawled between the sheets. He rolled over and lay there a moment. But he wasn't ready to go back under. He grabbed his cell phone to check his messages, but there was nothing from Sandra. Why would there be since he'd run her off earlier?

Then he remembered hearing the voices before he collapsed this afternoon. Sandra had been there, talking to his therapist. He winced, remembering how adamant he had been about not letting anybody in, about not wanting to talk to anybody or to see anybody. With a sinking heart, he guessed she had probably heard him.

And had taken it personally. Why wouldn't she? After everything else he had said and done, it *was* personal. He hadn't meant to hurt her. He didn't know for sure he had, but if that had been him on the other side of the door, and her in the bed, saying, *Keep them away, I don't want anyone in here*, he'd have taken it personally too.

Not in the mood to sleep right away, he sent her a text message. **Sorry I didn't see or talk to you earlier. I had a pretty rough day and went to bed. It's past midnight now, but I am awake. Still feeling like crap but better.**

Not giving himself a chance to second-guess his actions, he hit Send.

Chapter 16

HER PHONE WENT off. Sandra stared at it in the darkness. She shouldn't answer it. There was no need. Whoever was texting could wait until morning.

Only … she couldn't ignore it.

She snatched her phone off the night table and quickly checked to see who had sent her a message.

Cole.

Her heart stuttered, then stalled, and afterward raced ahead at the sight of his name. Of course he had her number. Every patient had the contact information for everyone on their team. So far, nobody had abused the system, so it worked well when somebody needed to contact them. She certainly hadn't expected a text at midnight though. She read his message and then sank back onto her bed.

Well, at least that lined up with what she had already overheard or assumed. She didn't understand quite what was going on, but he was still talking to her. She put down her phone and lay here in the darkness, wondering what she should do. She wanted to answer his text, but it might be better if she didn't.

When her phone chimed again, she was afraid to pick it up. It was Cole once more. This time, his message was simple.

I'm so sorry. I never meant to hurt you. I never

meant to get you in trouble.

There was something otherworldly about lying in bed, reading his communication, discerning what he meant by the words. Was there more to those statements? Was he saying, *Walk away*, that he didn't want anything to do with her? Or had he really had such a crappy day, and he hadn't done anything on purpose, so, if she'd been caught in the backlash, he was sorry?

She didn't know how to answer him or if she even wanted to. If she did reply, he'd know she was awake. Did she want that? She shook her head. She didn't know what the hell she wanted.

Wrong. She wanted her life back the way it was a few days ago, when she was in this little fantasy world that they were both working toward a relationship. Something other than friends. Something other than patient and practitioner. She already knew that could go very wrong. She thought back to what she'd heard today and to the therapist's words when they spoke outside Cole's room.

Cole had had a breakthrough, but what had he broken through from? If it was old traumas, that could be incredibly devastating. Any breakthrough was good because those walls were what stopped people from improving and from doing the things they needed to do. Things they had locked away and were afraid of that directed their actions as they moved forward. So much of it was painful. But it was old pain.

This was a different kind of growth. It was spiritual and emotional, and if he was doing that, more power to him. It said a lot about his character that he was taking those steps. Sometimes those changes happened when you least expected them. Like a paradigm shift, when suddenly you saw things and realized how you'd been acting or how you'd seen things. Realizing how very bad things had been or at least how very improved they were now.

She hated to use the words *good* and *bad* because that always came off as judgmental. That wasn't what she wanted for her patients or herself. But there was this awareness of life afterward. As a child, you stuffed everything down inside, but it still directed your actions or words and your life ever after. As you added more and more events, more painful conversations and hurtful words and actions by others that you couldn't face, they all determined who you ended up being.

She was only guessing here that something like that had happened to Cole. She already knew he was competitive and afraid of being compared and found lacking, always wanting to be the best. She didn't know what else was going on. But one thing she did know was that regardless of how it turned out, she could not do any less than she always did.

He had reached out to her. If she didn't reach back, it was a done deal. She wouldn't have to worry about whether they'd be the professional patient and practitioner. That relationship would be finished. If she did reach out, it was no guarantee of anything more, but at least it would help his healing. And that was ultimately what he was here for.

And what she was here for.

If she did nothing other than her best to get him back on his feet and to move him out the door, she could look back on this stage and smile and know what she'd done had been the best thing for him. It might not be the best thing for her, but that was not the point of her being here. The question was, was she a big enough person to reach out to Cole? She stared at the text message. He probably thought she was asleep and would see this when she woke up. Instead, she was lying in her bed, unable to sleep because of him. Quickly she tapped out a reply. **No need to apologize. Life happens.**

She knew that was rather cold, but if she was sending it from her practitioner's point of view, he had to know he was off the hook. She certainly didn't begrudge him anything. After his words to her earlier, she decided to make something better out of all this instead of the stupid back and forth texting.

Nothing held them apart but themselves. That made her angry. Because that truly meant he wasn't ready. She was, he wasn't, and that was her problem, so she had to walk away. She'd always prided herself on having forthright conversations instead of endless drama. She was not someone who played mind games and twisted up words, reading things into them. Yet, here she hadn't had that clean, clear conversation she was accustomed to.

That was as much on her shoulders as on his. He was a good guy. He'd had a rough start, but he'd also had a great number of years where he'd done well in life. It was a glaring example of reaching the top, enjoying success, and then having your feet pulled out from under you. In his case, having his feet pulled out from under him had resulted in the loss of a limb. He could certainly bounce back from that injury with absolutely no ongoing problems. The damaged muscle could be mended. The physical lifestyle would be harder. But all of it was doable. He could be and do and have anything he wanted. He just had to believe in it. He had to want it enough to make the effort to achieve it. She threw down her phone, rolled over and tried to go back to sleep.

Her phone beeped again. "Shit."

She stared at the damned thing flashing on her bed beside her. It was Cole again. Hesitantly she reached out and clicked on the text.

No, that's not life happening. That was me dealing with garbage. I think you heard something today that I didn't mean for you to. I wasn't sending you away, in particular. I wanted the world to go away. At least until I could restabilize and find my footing. Some old stuff came up today, and I let it all go, but in the process, it felt like I'd let go of my foundation. I was pretty shaky for a while. I was just trying to cocoon.

Her breath gusted out of her lungs in a big rush. She stared into the darkness around her. It was hard not to be affected by his words. Because she too knew how that felt. Anybody could relate to it. Anybody who lived and had a relationship, or who had tried to do something and failed. Life was as much about adjusting as it was about progressing. Sometimes it was the same thing. Accomplishments for patients at Hathaway House could be measured in minuscule increments.

It wasn't the same for much of the world. But when it came to emotional healing, no cryptic signposts said how well you were doing. Usually, when something major happened to break through a wall following a trauma, there was hell. For Cole, there was quicksand all around him and a sense of newness and fear because now he understood what he'd been doing. So how would he stop himself from doing it again?

Supposedly the new patient perspective helped. But not always. He had done so well, and yes, she had heard those words. She'd reacted out of fear. She had been afraid he didn't want anything to do with her. Afraid he was shoving her away.

But he was right in telling the world to go away.

Slowly she typed her reply. **Understandable. Hope you're feeling better.**

She hit Send. She wanted to say so much more—texting seemed so cold and formal. Even though she'd used very informal language, it was hard to reach out through this medium. She stared at the phone and wondered if she should hit Dial instead.

But they were both lying in their beds, and that was an intimacy she wasn't sure he was ready for. As she rethought her decision, her phone rang in her fingers, startling her. Sure enough, it was Cole. With a soft smile on her face, she answered. "Hello, Cole. Aren't you supposed to be asleep right now?" she chided gently.

"I could say the same for you," he said.

His voice was both pained and harsh, as if his throat was sore. He'd probably been crying. For men who cried rarely, their throats were often sore afterward. "Did you sleep all afternoon?"

"Yes. I missed dinner, and now I'm lying here, wondering how long it'll be until breakfast," he said, a touch of self-deprecation in his tone. "I slept so many hours already, I doubt I'm gonna sleep again tonight."

"After that kind of emotional trauma and release, you'd be surprised. You're awake now, but in another hour or so, you could be sound asleep again."

"I hope so." There was an awkward silence, and then he added, "I think you were in the hallway earlier. I didn't mean to name you specifically, but I thought it was you outside, and I didn't want you to see me that way. I was hurting. I was confused. And I was crying. I couldn't handle you seeing me like that."

He'd been afraid she'd view him differently because of

that. She shook her head wildly. "Oh Cole, I wouldn't think any less of you. Trauma is trauma. It doesn't matter if you're male or female, young or old. None of us are strong enough to bottle up everything life keeps throwing at us without reacting. I wouldn't have thought any less of you if I had seen you go through that breakthrough. You have to deal with the pain, the loss, or the sense of disconnect that often happens afterward. I certainly would never think any less of you if I saw you crying," she stated plainly. "Any more than I would want you to think less of me if our positions were reversed."

"Guys aren't supposed to ..." He fell silent.

"So it's okay for the so-called weaker sex to cry because we're supposedly less able to handle trauma? Because we supposedly cry at the drop of a hat?" She smiled as she thought how different the male and female psyches were. "I've seen many men cry, and all the more power to them. Much better to cry and let out that emotion than to bottle it up inside where it festers."

He gave a heavy sigh. "You're right. I couldn't deal with anything at the time."

"That was your right too. I did take it personally when I heard you say you didn't want anything to do with me and not to let me in. But then you've been acting strangely for a few days, and that was just one more blow."

She could almost hear the wince from his end of the phone. "I have a confession."

"What is it?" she asked slowly. She wasn't sure she wanted to hear this, but given that they were now talking honestly, she had to listen.

"The other day I walked around the floor, and I paused outside some offices to adjust my prosthetic as it's been giving me some trouble," he admitted. "I overheard a conversation about you. Something about a reprimand over me."

"Oh." She closed her eyes and reached up to pinch the bridge of her nose. "I'm sorry you heard that."

"It brought up all the times that I jumped too far, too fast, and fell. That up until that moment, I hadn't considered the impact my actions would have on anybody else, particularly you."

She shook her head, even though she knew he couldn't see her. "Don't worry about that. It wasn't even so much a reprimand as I made a change to our system because of that. I wasn't in trouble. I'm not in trouble. It's all fine."

He let out a breath, and even over the phone, she could hear the shaky tremor run through his exhale. He'd been worried about it.

"We mentioned it before briefly," he said. "But we never really discussed it, never went into the details of it. So, when I heard that, it brought up all my insecurities again. If we'd have spoken about it and if we'd have cleared the air the first time, then I could have brushed this off. But we didn't. Then today, with all that stuff that kept coming up, it seemed like this meeting was more punishment for you, and I didn't want to hurt you. Knowing you were in trouble over something I was responsible for—I couldn't deal with it."

She smiled. "Don't worry about any of that. Just focus on your healing."

"Yeah, I would, but my stomach is growling."

She chuckled. "If you want to meet on the deck, I'll see if I can rummage up some muffins and maybe something to drink. Hot milk or juice?"

There was silence for a long moment, and then he said,

"Can we?"

There was such hope in his voice she laughed out loud. "There are rules, but we're not prisoners. I'll get dressed, if you're up for it, and I'll meet you in the dining hall."

"Be there in ten," he said, and he rang off.

Her heart was lighter than she could've imagined when she had first laid down on her bed. She got up and quickly dressed in yoga pants and a light camisole top. Not sure how cold the night was outside, she grabbed a sweater and slipped on her flip-flops. She didn't have to get formal. It was midnight, after all. As she headed toward the eating area, she walked by the pool deck and thought of all the times she'd considered coming to the pool but hadn't. That would be a good idea tonight. It might help her fall asleep too. But first she'd spend a little time with Cole. Maybe they could patch up their relationship. If nothing else, her heart felt a whole lot lighter knowing he wasn't personally pushing her away.

COLE SLOWLY MADE his way through the dark hallways. A small series of running lights were along the edge of the hall, lighting up the floor so he wouldn't trip and fall. Although it was midnight, still the odd person wandered around. He avoided all the main areas and headed straight to the dining hall. He was still feeling pretty wrecked, but the thought of seeing Sandra right now, well, that was worth a lot.

He was grateful he'd reached out. He was even more grateful she'd responded. A quiet hum of activity came from the kitchen, and a few lights were on. He hadn't expected anything to be going on here at this hour but then realized a night staff was on duty. Maybe even kitchen staff, doing prep work or something. He didn't know. He did know there were a lot of people to feed, so it shouldn't be a surprise to learn about a night shift in the kitchen too. He wandered to the coffee island and studied the industrial-size maker. It was most likely the worst thing he should have right now.

"No coffee for you," Sandra said, her light voice coming out of the dim light. "I'll have a cup of herbal tea. What about you?"

"I haven't had warm milk since I was a kid," he said with a smile. "But hot chocolate might not be a bad idea."

She disappeared into the kitchen, with an air of somebody who lived here, worked here and knew the ins and outs way more than he did. He waited patiently until she came out again a few minutes later.

"One of the staff will deliver it to us," she said. "Let's go outside. I want to sit in the moonlight."

She walked ahead of him, leaving him to make his way behind her. He liked that about her. She didn't make any attempt to slow down. She walked normally and acted normally. It was up to him to become normal in the way he acted. There was a lot to be said for that.

Outside, the fresh air and moonlight made for a very special atmosphere. He stood there, absorbing the nighttime stillness, the silence broken by the odd chirp of a cricket or the croak of a bullfrog. The night was clear, and he could see the lights twinkling from the pool below. "I'd love to swim at this hour."

"The pool area isn't locked," she said. "But I'm not sure what the rules are for patients. I'm certainly allowed, as somebody who lives here and as part of the in-house staff." She shrugged. "We can check with Dani in the morning to see what the regulations are should you plan on swimming often at this time of night."

He nodded and took his place on one of the big benches that wrapped around the entire deck. "This is a good idea," he said. "Thank you for coming to meet with me."

"Thank you for texting me." She leaned forward. "Yesterday I'd just come to terms with whatever it is we were doing and needed to talk with you, which was why I was in the hallway outside your door. So, as for timing, it was pretty crappy on my part."

He winced. "Or rather crappy on my part."

She smiled. "But I'm fairly certain *this too shall pass.*"

He reached up and rubbed his eyes. "Like all this emotion. My eyes are hot and burning. My throat's dry and scratchy. My body aches in places that never ached before, even after Shane put it through all his workouts." Cole gave a half laugh. "Nobody warned me about this emotional and psychological stuff. I feel like somebody took a meat mallet and pounded me into the ground."

"That was actually *you,* doing that to yourself," she said cheerfully. "That was you pounding all that crap out of the recesses of your mind. In fact, you had to let it out. It's a principle in life that you find what you are, and who you are, in different places now."

He reached across to her and laid his hand on top of hers. "I don't want to think that I hurt our relationship."

He watched as she looked up in surprise, and then her gaze warmed. "That's what I came to talk to you about earlier," she confessed. "I was hoping we could get past whatever was going on between us and reach for something better."

He squeezed her fingers. "Yes, please."

He let go of her hand and settled back on the bench as

one of the kitchen staff came out with a tray. Not only was there hot chocolate for him but a variety of muffins and a couple pieces of fruit. He smiled. "Thank you very much. I was quite hungry."

The man nodded. "That'll happen when you miss dinner." He took the empty tray away and left the two of them in privacy.

Cole glanced at their surroundings. Nobody was in hearing distance. In fact, it appeared even the kitchen staff had left now. "It's really unique here when it's empty."

Sandra nodded. "The setting's very intimate right now."

He gave her a sideways smile. "Not intimate enough."

With that, she blushed in the shadows and gave a light laugh. "True."

As if that step of intimacy had been a little too far, too fast, they settled into a more general conversation. He shifted in his seat and finally said, "I feel like I don't know how to do anything anymore. You have to relearn everything in this situation, and things that I used to be good at, I have to start from the beginning again because apparently I'm no longer good at them."

She looked at him with a puzzled frown. "Like what?"

"Like flirting. Like having a relationship. Even basic day-to-day stuff."

She nodded. "I imagine that's because you see yourself as a very different person now, having to put your old skills together with the new body, and so far they probably don't fit for you."

"I don't want them to," he admitted. "I want to be the man who can get past this and reach for what he wants." Cole winced, knowing what her next question would be. Was he ready to answer it?

Maybe not but he wanted to. It felt like he'd been waiting all his life, playing catch-up and never getting what he truly wanted. And what he really wanted sat across from him right now. He didn't want to hurt her any more than he wanted there to be doubts between them. He didn't want to fail. He had to brave it out and tell her the truth.

She reached across and laid her hand, palm up, on the table. "What do you want?" she whispered.

He took a deep breath, gave her the most caring and loving smile he possibly could, grabbed her hand in his and whispered in the darkness, "You."

Chapter 17

TEARS CAME TO her eyes. How long had she waited to find a man who would care for her the way she cared for Cole? So many of her friends had partners, had dated men, and she'd been envious the whole time. She'd always wondered if her time would ever come. She wondered what was wrong with her, why she hadn't been attracted to any of them. Until Cole. It was all about Cole.

Still holding her hand, he asked, "Should I take that back?"

She looked up at him, startled at the tears pouring from her eyes. She sniffed them back and snatched one of the napkins off the table with her free hand, quickly wiping her eyes. "You can't take it back," she whispered. "You'd break my heart if you did."

He squeezed her hand so gently and slowly drew her inexorably closer. But the table was between them, so she got up and moved to stand at his side. Instead, he shifted on the bench and tucked her down until she sat in his lap. She snuggled in and wrapped her arms around his neck, simply holding him close.

"Are we past all that ugliness now?" she whispered.

"God, I hope so," he said. "I never wanted to hurt you. I never want to hurt you again. I'm a bit of a mess. I've still got lots to learn. I will get angry sometimes. There will be nights when I can't sleep because of the nightmares."

She reached up and placed a finger against his lips. "I know that. I understand that. I still want all of you anyway."

He crushed her to him. "You can't take that back either." He tilted her head up, so he could see the truth in her eyes. She held nothing back. They'd been at crosscurrents for too long. Somebody had to take the chance of being honest and open and walk across the water that separated them to the freedom that togetherness would bring.

He lowered his head and before he kissed her, he whispered, "Please don't take that back."

Then he crushed his lips against hers. Instantly passion rose between them. But a sweet, tender passion, more like the sealing of a promise. The tenderness of the kiss that meant forever. This wasn't about taking the moment just for them. This was about enjoying the moment as if it were the first of many more to come. She drew her arms tighter around his neck, holding on tightly. She couldn't think of anything she wanted more.

When he finally lifted his head, he asked, "Are you sure?"

She nodded and smiled. "I'm sure." She studied him and then gently dabbed away the moisture in the corners of his eyes. "Are you okay?"

He cuddled her close against him. "Never better. I've finally found what I've been racing toward. I finally understand why I have always been playing catch-up. Because they all had something I've never had. I didn't understand it until today. Now I finally do."

She leaned back, confusion in her gaze, having no idea what he was talking about. He stretched out a finger and tilted her chin up.

"They always had somebody to love them. They always had someone to love back. I never did. It seemed like, while they were in this loving and warm cocoon, I was out in the cold. Maybe since I had no family life to speak of, the SEALs became my family. But I always felt unloved. Felt I had no one to love me back."

He took a deep breath and whispered against her hair.

"Until you."

Epilogue

DENTON HAMILTON STARED at his email in disbelief. He'd heard so much about Hathaway House from Brock and Cole that Denton had been living in a fantasy world, hoping a miracle would happen and he'd have a chance to join his friends at the same center.

But the costs ... they were horrific.

He'd applied anyway. Made his case, knowing they took on a certain number of pro bono cases, and had hoped and waited.

He pulled out his cell phone and called Brock. It rang several times, then went to voice mail. He tried Cole.

"Denton, what's up?"

The curiosity in his friend's voice was justified. They'd been on the phone only a few minutes earlier. "I got in," Denton croaked, his voice clogging up. He cleared his throat several times, then repeated, "I got into Hathaway House. They have a bed for me." His voice rose at the end as the words in front of him finally settled in. "I'm coming there, Cole. I'll be there next week. We'll be together again."

"Holy crap, are you serious? That's the best news I've heard in a long time," Cole said warmly. "Wait until you see this place. You'll love it." He paused, then added in a teasing voice, "And you'll love the women."

"Nah, I'm not coming there for that. Besides, just because you and Brock found the perfect ladies for your lives, that doesn't mean Cupid is smiling in my direction. No, I'm happy to know I'm coming to Hathaway House and getting my best chance at regaining my strength and my health."

"Maybe so, but in this place, miracles do happen. I got mine. I know there is one here just for you."

This concludes Book 3 of Hathaway House: Cole.

Read about Denton: Hathaway House, Book 4

Hathaway House: Denton (Book #4)

Welcome to Hathaway House. Rehab Center. Safe Haven. Second chance at life and love.

Navy SEAL Denton Hamilton has checked himself into Hathaway House, hoping for a fraction of the results his friends have gotten at the rehab center. Now missing a rib, muscles and a portion of his stomach, as well as suffering from PTSD, Denton would be happy to have his physical self healed. He's not so sure he'll ever get his mental health back, and finding a woman who'll have him now—as his friends have been lucky enough to do—is out of the question. Who would be willing to love a man like him?

Administrative Assistant Hannah Forsythe helps Dani run Hathaway House. A loner at heart, she's drawn to Denton's struggle and dismayed at his belief that no one could ever love him. But when an ill-advised observation she makes has unexpected consequences for Denton's recovery, Hannah's only choice is to separate herself from him to help him progress without her.

As time passes, Hannah wonders if her choice has cost her everything she's ever wanted or whether Denton can work through his feelings to give them both their happy ending at Hathaway House.

Book 4 is available now!

To find out more visit Dale Mayer's website.

http://smarturl.it/DentonDMUniversal

Author's Note

Thank you for reading Cole: Hathaway House, Book 3! If you enjoyed the book, please take a moment and leave a short review.

Dear reader,

I love to hear from readers, and you can contact me at my website: www.dalemayer.com or at my Facebook author page. To be informed of new releases and special offers, sign up for my newsletter or follow me on BookBub. And if you are interested in joining Dale Mayer's Reader Group, here is the Facebook sign up page.
facebook.com/groups/402384989872660

Cheers,
Dale Mayer

Get THREE Free Books Now!

Have you met the SEALS of Honor?

SEALs of Honor Books 1, 2, and 3. Follow the stories of brave, badass warriors who serve their country with honor and love their women to the limits of life and death.

Read Mason, Hawk, and Dane right now for FREE.

Go here and tell me where to send them!
http://smarturl.it/EthanBofB

About the Author

Dale Mayer is a USA Today bestselling author best known for her Psychic Visions and Family Blood Ties series. Her contemporary romances are raw and full of passion and emotion (Second Chances, SKIN), her thrillers will keep you guessing (By Death series), and her romantic comedies will keep you giggling (It's a Dog's Life and Charmin Marvin Romantic Comedy series).

She honors the stories that come to her – and some of them are crazy and break all the rules and cross multiple genres!

To go with her fiction, she also writes nonfiction in many different fields with books available on resume writing, companion gardening and the US mortgage system. She has recently published her Career Essentials Series. All her books are available in print and ebook format.

Connect with Dale Mayer Online

Dale's Website – www.dalemayer.com
Twitter – @DaleMayer
Facebook – dalemayer.com/fb
BookBub – bookbub.com/authors/dale-mayer

Also by Dale Mayer

Published Adult Books:

Hathaway House
Aaron, Book 1
Brock, Book 2
Cole, Book 3
Denton, Book 4
Elliot, Book 5
Finn, Book 6

The K9 Files
Ethan, Book 1
Pierce, Book 2
Zane, Book 3
Blaze, Book 4
Lucas, Book 5
Parker, Book 6
Carter, Book 7

Lovely Lethal Gardens
Arsenic in the Azaleas, Book 1
Bones in the Begonias, Book 2
Corpse in the Carnations, Book 3
Daggers in the Dahlias, Book 4
Evidence in the Echinacea, Book 5
Footprints in the Ferns, Book 6

Psychic Vision Series
Tuesday's Child
Hide 'n Go Seek
Maddy's Floor
Garden of Sorrow
Knock Knock...
Rare Find
Eyes to the Soul
Now You See Her
Shattered
Into the Abyss
Seeds of Malice
Eye of the Falcon
Itsy-Bitsy Spider
Unmasked
Deep Beneath
From the Ashes
Psychic Visions Books 1–3
Psychic Visions Books 4–6
Psychic Visions Books 7–9

By Death Series
Touched by Death
Haunted by Death
Chilled by Death
By Death Books 1–3

Broken Protocols – Romantic Comedy Series
Cat's Meow
Cat's Pajamas
Cat's Cradle
Cat's Claus
Broken Protocols 1-4

Broken and... Mending

Skin
Scars
Scales (of Justice)
Broken but... Mending 1-3

Glory

Genesis
Tori
Celeste
Glory Trilogy

Biker Blues

Morgan: Biker Blues, Volume 1
Cash: Biker Blues, Volume 2

SEALs of Honor

Mason: SEALs of Honor, Book 1
Hawk: SEALs of Honor, Book 2
Dane: SEALs of Honor, Book 3
Swede: SEALs of Honor, Book 4
Shadow: SEALs of Honor, Book 5
Cooper: SEALs of Honor, Book 6
Markus: SEALs of Honor, Book 7
Evan: SEALs of Honor, Book 8
Mason's Wish: SEALs of Honor, Book 9
Chase: SEALs of Honor, Book 10
Brett: SEALs of Honor, Book 11
Devlin: SEALs of Honor, Book 12
Easton: SEALs of Honor, Book 13
Ryder: SEALs of Honor, Book 14
Macklin: SEALs of Honor, Book 15
Corey: SEALs of Honor, Book 16

Heroes for Hire

Vince's Vixen: Heroes for Hire, Book 19
Heroes for Hire, Books 1–3
Heroes for Hire, Books 4–6
Heroes for Hire, Books 7–9
Heroes for Hire, Books 10–12
Heroes for Hire, Books 13–15

SEALs of Steel
Badger: SEALs of Steel, Book 1
Erick: SEALs of Steel, Book 2
Cade: SEALs of Steel, Book 3
Talon: SEALs of Steel, Book 4
Laszlo: SEALs of Steel, Book 5
Geir: SEALs of Steel, Book 6
Jager: SEALs of Steel, Book 7
The Final Reveal: SEALs of Steel, Book 8
SEALs of Steel, Books 1–4
SEALs of Steel, Books 5–8
SEALs of Steel, Books 1–8

Collections
Dare to Be You...
Dare to Love...
Dare to be Strong...
RomanceX3

Standalone Novellas
It's a Dog's Life
Riana's Revenge
Second Chances

Published Young Adult Books:

Family Blood Ties Series
Vampire in Denial
Vampire in Distress
Vampire in Design
Vampire in Deceit
Vampire in Defiance
Vampire in Conflict
Vampire in Chaos
Vampire in Crisis
Vampire in Control
Vampire in Charge
Family Blood Ties Set 1–3
Family Blood Ties Set 1–5
Family Blood Ties Set 4–6
Family Blood Ties Set 7–9
Sian's Solution, A Family Blood Ties Series Prequel
    Novelette

Design series
Dangerous Designs
Deadly Designs
Darkest Designs
Design Series Trilogy

Standalone
In Cassie's Corner
Gem Stone (a Gemma Stone Mystery)
Time Thieves

Published Non-Fiction Books:

Career Essentials
Career Essentials: The Résumé
Career Essentials: The Cover Letter
Career Essentials: The Interview
Career Essentials: 3 in 1

CPSIA information can be obtained
at www.ICGtesting.com
Printed in the USA
LVHW031517021019
632974LV00010B/765/P